A STRANGE DISAPPEARANCE

LECTOR HOUSE PUBLIC DOMAIN WORKS

A STRANGE DISAPPEARANCE

ANNA KATHARINE GREEN

ISBN: 978-93-5342-086-4

First Published: -

LECTOR HOUSE LLP
E-MAIL: lectorpublishing@gmail.com

A STRANGE DISAPPEARANCE

BY

ANNA KATHARINE GREEN

CONTENTS

A STRANGE DISAPPEARANCE

CHAPTER I.

A NOVEL CASE

"Talking of sudden disappearances the one you mention of Hannah in that Leavenworth case of ours, is not the only remarkable one which has come under my direct notice. Indeed, I know of another that in some respects, at least, surpasses that in points of interest, and if you will promise not to inquire into the real names of the parties concerned, as the affair is a secret, I will relate you my experience regarding it."

The speaker was Q, the rising young detective, universally acknowledged by us of the force as the most astute man for mysterious and unprecedented cases, then in the bureau, always and of course excepting Mr. Gryce; and such a statement from him could not but arouse our deepest curiosity. Drawing up, then, to the stove around which we were sitting in lazy enjoyment of one of those off-hours so dear to a detective's heart, we gave with alacrity the required promise; and settling himself back with the satisfied air of a man who has a good story to tell that does not entirely lack certain points redounding to his own credit, he began:

I was one Sunday morning loitering at the — —- Precinct Station, when the door opened and a respectable-looking middle-aged woman came in, whose agitated air at once attracted my attention. Going up to her, I asked her what she wanted.

"A detective," she replied, glancing cautiously about on the faces of the various men scattered through the room. "I don't wish anything said about it, but a girl disappeared from our house last night, and"—she stopped here, her emotion seeming to choke her—"and I want some one to look her up," she went on at last with the most intense emphasis.

"A girl? what kind of a girl; and what house do you mean when you say our house?"

She looked at me keenly before replying. "You are a young man," said she; "isn't there some one here more responsible than yourself that I can talk to?"

I shrugged my shoulders and beckoned to Mr. Gryce who was just then passing. She at once seemed to put confidence in him. Drawing him aside, she whispered a few low eager words which I could not hear. He listened nonchalantly for a moment but suddenly made a move which I knew indicated strong and surprised interest, though from his face—but you know what Gryce's face is. I was about to walk off, convinced he had got hold of something he would prefer to manage himself, when the Superintendent came in.

"Where is Gryce?" asked he; "tell him I want him."

Mr. Gryce heard him and hastened forward. As he passed me, he whispered, "Take a man and go with this woman; look into matters and send me word if you want me; I will be here for two hours."

I did not need a second permission. Beckoning to Harris, I reapproached the woman. "Where do you come from," said I, "I am to go back with you and investigate the affair it seems."

"Did he say so?" she asked, pointing to Mr. Gryce who now stood with his back to us busily talking with the Superintendent.

I nodded, and she at once moved towards the door. "I come from No.— — Second Avenue: Mr. Blake's house," she whispered, uttering a name so well known, I at once understood Mr. Gryce's movement of sudden interest "A girl—one who sewed for us—disappeared last night in a way to alarm us very much. She was taken from her room—" "Yes," she cried vehemently, seeing my look of sarcastic incredulity, "taken from her room; she never went of her own accord; and she must be found if I spend every dollar of the pittance I have laid up in the bank against my old age."

Her manner was so intense, her tone so marked and her words so vehement, I at once and naturally asked if the girl was a relative of hers that she felt her abduction so keenly.

"No," she replied, "not a relative, but," she went on, looking every way but in my face, "a very dear friend—a—a—protegee, I think they call it, of mine; I—I— She must be found," she again reiterated.

We were by this time in the street.

"Nothing must be said about it," she now whispered, catching me by the arm. "I told him so," nodding back to the building from which we had just issued, "and he promised secrecy. It can be done without folks knowing anything about it, can't it?"

"What?" I asked.

"Finding the girl."

"Well," said I, "we can tell you better about that when we know a few more of the facts. What is the girl's name and what makes you think she didn't go out of the house-door of her own accord?"

"Why, why, everything. She wasn't the person to do it; then the looks of her room, and—They all got out of the window," she cried suddenly, "and went away by the side gate into — — — Street."

"They? Who do you mean by they?"

"Why, whoever they were who carried her off."

I could not suppress the "bah!" that rose to my lips. Mr. Gryce might have been able to, but I am not Gryce.

"You don't believe," said she, "that she was carried off?"

"Well, no," said I, "not in the sense you mean."

She gave another nod back to the police station now a block or so distant. "He did'nt seem to doubt it at all."

I laughed. "Did you tell him you thought she had been taken off in this way?"

"Yes, and he said, 'Very likely.' And well he might, for I heard the men talking in her room, and—"

"You heard men talking in her room—when?"

"O, it must have been as late as half-past twelve. I had been asleep and the noise they made whispering, woke me."

"Wait," I said, "tell me where her room is, hers and yours."

"Hers is the third story back, mine the front one on the same floor."

"Who are you?" I now inquired. "What position do you occupy in Mr. Blake's house?"

"I am the housekeeper."

Mr. Blake was a bachelor.

"And you were wakened last night by hearing whispering which seemed to come from this girl's room."

"Yes, I at first thought it was the folks next door,—we often hear them when they are unusually noisy,—but soon I became assured it came from her room; and more astonished than I could say,—She is a good girl," she broke in, suddenly looking at me with hotly indignant eyes, "a—a—as good a girl as this whole city can show; don't you dare, any of you, to hint at anything else o—"

"Come, come," I said soothingly, a little ashamed of my too communicative face, "I haven't said anything, we will take it for granted she is as good as gold, go on."

The woman wiped her forehead with a hand that trembled like a leaf. "Where was I?" said she. "O, I heard voices and was surprised and got up and went to her door. The noise I made unlocking my own must have startled her, for all was perfectly quiet when I got there. I waited a moment, then I turned the knob and called her: she did not reply and I called again. Then she came to the door, but did not unlock it. 'What is it?' she asked. 'O,' said I, 'I thought I heard talking here and I was frightened,' 'It must have been next door,' said she. I begged pardon and went back to my room. There was no more noise, but when in the morning we broke into her room and found her gone, the window open and signs of distress and struggle around, I knew I had not been mistaken; that there were men with her when I went to her door, and that they had carried her off—"

This time I could not restrain myself.

"Did they drop her out of the window?" I inquired.

"O," said she, "we are building an extension, and there is a ladder running up to the third floor, and it was by means of that they took her."

"Indeed! she seems at least to have been a willing victim," I remarked.

The woman clutched my arm with a grip like iron. "Don't you believe it," gasped she, stopping me in the street where we were. "I tell you if what I say is true, and these burglars or whatever they were, did carry her off, it was an agony to her, an awful, awful thing that will kill her if it has not done so already. You don't know what you are talking about, you never saw her—"

"Was she pretty," I asked, hurrying the woman along, for more than one passer-by had turned their heads to look at us. The question seemed in some way to give her a shock.

"Ah, I don't know," she muttered; "some might not think so, I always did; it depended upon the way you looked at her."

For the first time I felt a thrill of anticipation shoot through my veins. Why, I could not say. Her tone was peculiar, and she spoke in a sort of brooding way as though she were weighing something in her own mind; but then her manner had been peculiar throughout. Whatever it was that aroused my suspicion, I determined henceforth to keep a very sharp eye upon her ladyship. Levelling a straight glance at her face, I asked her how it was that she came to be the one to inform the authorities of the girl's disappearance.

"Doesn't Mr. Blake know anything about it?"

The faintest shadow of a change came into her manner. "Yes," said she, "I told him at breakfast time; but Mr. Blake doesn't take much interest in his servants; he leaves all such matters to me."

"Then he does not know you have come for the police?"

"No, sir, and O, if you would be so good as to keep it from him. It is not necessary he should know. I shall let you in the back way. Mr. Blake is a man who never meddles with anything, and—"

"What did Mr. Blake say this morning when you told him that this girl—By the way, what is her name?"

"Emily."

"That this girl, Emily, had disappeared during the night?"

"Not much of anything, sir. He was sitting at the breakfast table reading his paper, he merely looked up, frowned a little in an absent-minded way, and told me I must manage the servants' affairs without troubling him."

"And you let it drop?"

"Yes sir; Mr. Blake is not a man to speak twice to."

I could easily believe that from what I had seen of him in public, for though by no means a harsh looking man, he had a reserved air which if maintained in private must have made him very difficult of approach.

We were now within a half block or so of the old-fashioned mansion regarded by this scion of New York's aristocracy as one of the most desirable residences in the city; so motioning to the man who had accompanied me to take his stand in a doorway near by and watch for the signal I would give him in case I wanted Mr. Gryce, I turned to the woman, who was now all in a flutter, and asked her how she proposed to get me into the house without the knowledge of Mr. Blake.

"O sir, all you have got to do is to follow me right up the back stairs; he won't notice, or if he does will not ask any questions."

And having by this time reached the basement door, she took out a key from her pocket and inserting it in the lock, at once admitted us into the dwelling.

CHAPTER II.

A FEW POINTS

Mrs. Daniels, for that was her name, took me at once up stairs to the third story back room. As we passed through the halls, I could not but notice how rich, though sombre were the old fashioned walls and heavily frescoed ceilings, so different in style and coloring from what we see now-a-days in our secret penetrations into Fifth Avenue mansions. Many as are the wealthy houses I have been called upon to enter in the line of my profession, I had never crossed the threshold of such an one as this before, and impervious as I am to any foolish sentimentalities, I felt a certain degree of awe at the thought of invading with police investigation, this home of ancient Knicker-bocker respectability. But once in the room of the missing girl, every consideration fled save that of professional pride and curiosity. For almost at first blush, I saw that whether Mrs. Daniels was correct or not in her surmises as to the manner of the girl's disappearance, the fact that she had disappeared was likely to prove an affair of some importance. For, let me state the facts in the order in which I noticed them. The first thing that impressed me was, that whatever Mrs. Daniels called her, this was no sewing girl's room into which I now stepped. Plain as was the furniture in comparison with the elaborate richness of the walls and ceiling, there were still scattered through the room, which was large even for a thirty foot house, articles of sufficient elegance to make the supposition that it was the abode of an ordinary seamstress open to suspicion, if no more.

Mrs. Daniels, seeing my look of surprise, hastened to provide some explanation. "It is the room which has always been devoted to sewing," said she; "and when Emily came, I thought it would be easier to put up a bed here than to send her upstairs. She was a very nice girl and disarranged nothing."

I glanced around on the writing-case lying open on a small table in the centre of the room, on the vase half full of partly withered roses, on the mantel-piece, the Shakespeare, and Macaulay's History lying on the stand at my right, thought my own thoughts, but said nothing.

"You found the door locked this morning?" asked I, after a moment's scrutiny of the room in which three facts had become manifest: first, that the girl had not occupied the bed the night before; second, that there had been some sort of struggle or surprise,—one of the curtains being violently torn as if grasped by an agitated hand, to say nothing of a chair lying upset on the floor with one of its legs broken; third, that the departure, strange as it may seem, had been by the window.

"Yes," returned she; "but there is a passageway leading from my room to hers and it was by that means we entered. There was a chair placed against the door on this side but we easily pushed it away."

I stepped to the window and looked out. Ah, it would not be so very difficult for a man to gain the street from that spot in a dark night, for the roof of the newly-erected extension was almost on a level with the window.

"Well," said she anxiously, "couldn't she have been got out that way?"

"More difficult things have been done," said I; and was about to step out upon the roof when I bethought to inquire of Mrs. Daniels if any of the girl's clothing was missing.

She immediately flew to the closets and thence to bureau drawers which she turned hastily over. "No, nothing is missing but a hat and cloak and—" She paused confusedly.

"And what?" I asked.

"Nothing," returned she, hurriedly closing the bureau drawer; "only some little knick-knacks."

"Knick-knacks!" quoth I. "If she stopped for knick-knacks, she couldn't have gone in any very unwilling frame of mind." And somewhat disgusted, I was about to throw up the whole affair and leave the room. But the indecision in Mrs. Daniels' own face deterred me.

"I don't understand it," murmured she, drawing her hand across her eyes. "I don't understand it. But," she went on with even an increase in her old tone of heart-felt conviction, "no matter whether we understand it or not, the case is serious; I tell you so, and she must be found."

I resolved to know the nature of that must, used as few women in her position would use it even under circumstances to all appearance more aggravated than these.

"Why, must?" said I. "If the girl went of her own accord as some things seem to show, why should you, no relative as you acknowledge, take the matter so to heart as to insist she shall be followed and brought back?"

She turned away, uneasily taking up and putting down some little matters on the table before her. "Is it not enough that I promise to pay for all expenses which a search will occasion, without my being forced to declare just why I should be willing to do so? Am I bound to tell you I love the girl? that I believe she has been taken away by foul means, and that to her great suffering and distress? that being fond of her and believing this, I am conscientious enough to put every means I possess at the command of those who will recover her?"

I was not satisfied with this but on that very account felt my enthusiasm revive.

"But Mr. Blake? Surely he is the one to take this interest if anybody."

"I have before said," returned she, paling however as she spoke, "that Mr. Blake takes very little interest in his servants."

I cast another glance about the room. "How long have you been in this house?" asked I.

"I was in the service of Mr. Blake's father and he died a year ago."

"Since when you have remained with Mr. Blake himself?"

"Yes sir."

"And this Emily, when did she come here?"

"Oh it must be eleven months or so ago."

"An Irish girl?"

"O no, American. She is not a common person, sir."

"What do you mean by that? That she was educated, lady-like, pretty, or what?"

"I don't know what to say. She was educated, yes, but not as you would call a lady educated. Yet she knew a great many things the rest of us did'nt. She liked to read, you see, and—O sir, ask the girls about her, I never know what to say when I am questioned."

I scanned the gray-haired woman still more intently than I had yet done. Was she the weak common-place creature she seemed, or had she really some cause other than appeared for these her numerous breaks and hesitations.

"Where did you get this girl?" I inquired. "Where did she live before coming here?"

"I cannot say, I never asked her to talk about herself. She came to me for work and I liked her and took her without recommendation."

"And she has served you well?"

"Excellently."

"Been out much? Had any visitors?"

She shook her head. "Never went out and never had any visitors."

I own I was nonplussed, "Well," said I, "no more of this at present. I must first find out if she left this house alone or in company with others." And without further parley I stepped out upon the roof of the extension.

As I did so I debated with myself whether the case warranted me or not in sending for Mr. Gryce. As yet there was nothing to show that the girl had come to any harm. A mere elopement with or without a lover to help her, was not such a serious matter that the whole police force need be stirred up on the subject; and if the woman had money, as she said, ready to give the man who should discover the whereabouts of this girl, why need that money be divided up any more than was necessary. Yet Gryce was not one to be dallied with. He had said, send for him if the affair seemed to call for his judgment, and somehow the affair did promise to be a trifle complicated. I was yet undetermined when I reached the edge of the roof.

It was a dizzy descent, but once made, escape from the yard beneath would be easy. A man could take that road without difficulty; but a woman! Baffled at the idea I turned thoughtfully back, when I beheld something on the roof before me that caused me to pause and ask myself if this was going to turn out to be a tragedy after all. It was a drop of congealed blood. Further on towards the window was another, and yes, further still, another and another. I even found one upon the very window ledge itself. Bounding into the room, I searched the carpet for further traces. It was the worst one in the world to find anything upon of the nature of which I was seeking, being a confused pattern of mingled drab and red, and in my difficulty I had to stoop very low.

"What are you looking for?" cried Mrs. Daniels.

I pointed to the drop on the window sill. "Do you see that?" I asked.

She uttered an exclamation and bent nearer. "Blood!" cried she, and stood staring, with rapidly paling cheeks and trembling form. "They have killed her and he will never—"

As she did not finish I looked up.

"Do you think it was her blood?" she whispered in a horrified tone.

"There is every reason to believe so," rejoined I, pointing to a spot where I had at last discovered not only one crimson drop but many, scattered over the scarcely redder roses under my feet.

"Ah, it is worse than I thought," murmured she. "What are you going to do? What can we do?

"I am going to send for another detective," returned I; and stepping to the window I telegraphed at once to the man Harris to go for Mr. Gryce.

"The one we saw at the Station?"

I bowed assent.

Her face lost something of its drawn expression. "O I am glad; he will do something."

Subduing my indignation at this back thrust, I employed my time in taking note of such details as had escaped my previous attention. They were not many. The open writing-desk—in which, however I found no letters or written documents of any kind, only a few sheets of paper, with pen, ink, etc.; the brush and hairpins scattered on the bureau as though the girl had been interrupted while arranging her hair (if she had been interrupted); and the absence of any great pile of work such as one would expect to see in a room set apart for sewing, were all I could discover. Not much to help us, in case this was to prove an affair of importance as I began to suspect.

With Mr. Gryce's arrival, however, things soon assumed a better shape. He came to the basement door, was ushered in by your humble servant, had the whole matter as far as I had investigated it, at his finger-ends in a moment, and was upstairs and in that room before I, who am called the quickest man in the force as you all know, could have time to determine just what difference his presence would make to me in a pecuniary way in event of Mrs. Daniels' promises amounting to anything. He did not remain there long, but when he came down I saw that his interest was in no wise lessened.

"What kind of a looking girl was this?" he asked, hurrying up to Mrs. Daniels who had withdrawn into a recess in the lower hall while all this was going on. "Describe her to me, hair, eyes, complexion, etc.; you know."

"I—I—don't know as I can," she stammered reluctantly, turning very red in the face. "I am a poor one for noticing. I will call one of the girls, I—" She was gone before we realized she had not finished her sentence.

"Humph!" broke from Mr. Gryce's lips as he thoughtfully took down a vase that stood on a bracket near by and looked into it.

I did not venture a word.

When Mrs. Daniels came back she had with her a trim-looking girl of prepossessing appearance.

"This is Fanny," said she; "she knows Emily well, being in the habit of waiting on her at table; she will tell you what you want to hear. I have explained to her," she went on, nodding towards Mr. Gryce with a composure such as she had not before displayed; "that you are looking for your niece who ran away from home some time ago to go into some sort of service."

"Certainly, ma'am," quoth that gentleman, bowing with mock admiration to the gas-fixture. Then carelessly shifting his glance to the cleaning-cloth which Fanny held rather conspicuously in her hand, he repeated the question he had already put to Mrs. Daniels.

The girl, tossing her head just a trifle, at once replied:

"O she was good-looking enough, if that is what you mean, for them as likes a girl with cheeks as white as this cloth was afore I rubbed the spoons with it. As for her eyes, they was blacker than her hair, which was the blackest I ever see. She had no flesh at all, and as for her figure—" Fanny glanced down on her own well developed person, and gave a shrug inexpressibly suggestive.

"Is this description true?" Mr. Gryce asked, seemingly of Mrs. Daniels, though his gaze rested with curious intentness on the girl's head which was covered with a little cap.

"Sufficiently so," returned Mrs. Daniels in a very low tone, however. Then with a sudden display of energy, "Emily's figure is not what you would call plump. I have seen her—" She broke off as if a little startled at herself and motioned Fanny to go.

"Wait a moment," interposed Mr. Gryce in his soft way. "You said the girl's hair and eyes were dark; were they darker than yours?"

"O, yes sir;" replied the girl simpering, as she settled the ribbons on her cap.

"Let me see your hair."

She took off her cap with a smile.

"Ha, very pretty, very pretty. And the other girls? You have other girls I suppose?"

"Two, sir;" returned Mrs. Daniels.

"How about their complexions? Are they lighter too than Emily's?"

"Yes, sir; about like Fanny's."

Mr. Gryce spread his hand over his breast in a way that assured me of his satisfaction, and allowed the girl to go.

"We will now proceed to the yard," said he. But at that moment the door of the front room opened and a gentleman stepped leisurely into the hall, whom at first glance I recognized as the master of the house. He was dressed for the street and had his hat in his hand. At the sight we all stood silent, Mrs. Daniels flushing up to the roots of her gray hair.

Mr. Blake is an elegant-looking man as you perhaps know; proud, reserved, and a trifle sombre. As he turned to come towards us, the light shining through the windows at our right, fell full upon his face, revealing such a self-absorbed and melancholy expression, I involuntarily drew back as if I had unwittingly intruded upon a great man's privacy. Mr. Gryce on the contrary stepped forward.

"Mr. Blake, I believe," said he, bowing in that deferential way he knows so well how to assume.

The gentleman, startled as it evidently seemed from a reverie, looked hastily up. Meeting Mr. Gryce's bland smile, he returned the bow, but haughtily, and as it appeared in an abstracted way.

"Allow me to introduce myself," proceeded my superior. "I am Mr. Gryce from the detective bureau. We were notified this morning that a girl in your employ had disappeared from your house last night in a somewhat strange and unusual way, and I just stepped over with my man here, to see if the matter is of sufficient importance to inquire into. With many apologies for the intrusion, I stand obedient to your orders."

With a frown expressive of annoyance, Mr. Blake glanced around and detecting Mrs. Daniels, said: "Did you consider the affair so serious as that?"

She nodded, seeming to find it difficult to speak.

He remained looking at her with an expression of some doubt. "I can hardly think," said he, "such extreme measures were necessary; the girl will doubtless come back, or if not—" His shoulders gave a slight shrug and he took out his gloves.

"The difficulty seems to be," quoth Mr. Gryce eyeing those gloves with his most intent and concentrated look, "that the girl did not go alone, but was helped away, or forced away, by parties who had previously broken into your house."

"That is a strange circumstance," remarked Mr. Blake, but still without any appearance of interest, "and if you are sure of what you say, demands, perhaps, some inquiry. I would not wish to put anything in the way of justice succoring the injured. But—" again he gave that slight shrug of the shoulders, indicative of doubt, if not indifference.

Mrs. Daniels trembled, and took a step forward. I thought she was going to speak, but instead of that she drew back again in her strange hesitating way.

Mr. Gryce did not seem to notice.

"Perhaps sir," said he, "if you will step upstairs with me to the room occupied by this girl, I may be able to show you certain evidences which will convince you that our errand here is not one of presumption."

"I am ready to concede that without troubling myself with proof," observed the master of the house with the faintest show of asperity. "Yet if there is anything to see of a startling nature, perhaps I had best yield to your wishes. Whereabouts in the house is this girl's room, Mrs. Daniels?"

"It is—I gave her the third story back, Mr. Blake;" replied that woman, nervously eyeing his face. "It was large and light for sewing, and she was so nice—"

He impatiently waved his hand on which he had by this time fitted his glove to a nicety, as if these details were an unnecessary bore to him, and motioned her to show the way. Instantly a new feeling appeared to seize her, that of alarm.

"I hardly think you need trouble Mr. Blake to go up-stairs," she murmured, turning towards Mr. Gryce. "I am sure when you tell him the curtains were torn, and the chair upset, the window open and—"

But Mr. Gryce was already on the stairs with Mr. Blake, whom this small opposition seemed to have at once determined.

"O my God!" she murmured to herself, "who could have foreseen this." And ignoring my presence with all the egotism of extreme agitation, she hurried past me to the room above, where I speedily joined her.

CHAPTER III.

THE CONTENTS OF A BUREAU DRAWER

Mr. Blake was standing in the centre of the room when I entered, carelessly following with his eyes the motion of Mr. Gryce's finger as that gentleman pointed with unwearying assiduity to the various little details that had struck us. His hat was still in his hand, and he presented a very formidable and imposing appearance, or so Mrs. Daniels appeared to think as she stood watching him from the corner, whither she had withdrawn herself.

"A forcible departure you see," exclaimed Mr. Gryce; "she had not even time to gather up her clothes;" and with a sudden movement he stooped and pulled out one of the bureau drawers before the eyes of his nonchalant listener.

Immediately a smothered exclamation struck our ears, and Mrs. Daniels started forward.

"I pray, gentlemen," she entreated, advancing in such a way as to place herself against the front of the bureau in a manner to preclude the opening of any more drawers, "that you will remember that a modest woman such as this girl was, would hardly like to have her clothing displayed before the eyes of strangers."

Mr. Gryce instantly closed the drawer.

"You are right," said he; "pardon the rough ways of a somewhat hardened officer of the law."

She drew up closer to the bureau, still protecting it with her meagre but energetic form while her eyes rested with almost a savage expression upon the master of the house as if he, and not the detective, had been the aggressor whose advances she feared.

Mr. Blake did not return the look.

"If that is all you can show me, I think I will proceed to my appointment," said he. "The matter does seem to be more serious than I thought, and if you judge it necessary to take any active measures, why, let no consideration of my great and inherent dislike to notoriety of any kind, interfere with what you consider your duty. As for the house, it is at your command, under Mrs. Daniels' direction. Good morning." And returning our bows with one singularly impressive for all its elegant carelessness, he at once withdrew.

Mrs. Daniels took one long deep breath and came from the bureau. Instantly Mr. Gryce stooped and pulled out the drawer she had so visibly protected. A white towel met our eyes, spread neatly out at its full length. Lifting it, we looked beneath. A carefully folded dress of dark blue silk, to all appearance elegantly made, confronted our rather eager eyes. Beside it, a collar of exquisite lace—I know enough of such matters to be a judge—pricked through by a gold breast-pin of a strange and unique pattern. A withered bunch of what appeared to have been a bouquet of red roses, surmounted the whole, giving to the otherwise common-place collection the appearance of a relic from the tomb.

We both drew back in some amazement, involuntarily glancing up at Mrs. Daniels.

"I have no explanation to give," said that woman, with a calmness strangely in contrast to the agitation she had displayed while Mr. Blake had remained in the room. "That those things rich as they are, really belonged to the girl, I have no doubt. She brought them when she came, and they only confirm what I have before intimated: that she was no ordinary sewing girl, but a woman who had seen better days."

With a low "humph!" and another glance at the dark blue dress and delicate collar, Mr. Gryce carefully replaced the cloth he had taken from them, and softly closed the drawer without either of us having laid a finger upon a single article. Five minutes later he disappeared from the room.

I did not see him again till occasion took me below, when I beheld him softly issue from Mr. Blake's private apartment. Meeting me, he smiled, and I saw that whether he was conscious of betraying it or not, he had come upon some clue or at the least fashioned for himself some theory with which he was more or less satisfied.

"An elegant apartment, that," whispered he, nodding sideways toward the room he had just left, "pity you haven't time to examine it."

"Are you sure that I haven't?" returned I, drawing a step nearer to escape the eyes of Mrs. Daniels who had descended after me.

"Quite sure;" and we hastened down together into the yard.

But my curiosity once aroused in this way would not let me rest. Taking an opportunity when Mr. Gryce was engaged in banter with the girls below, and in this way learning more in a minute of what he wanted to know than some men would gather in an hour by that or any other method, I stole lightly back and entered this room.

I almost started in my surprise. Instead of the luxurious apartment I had prepared myself to behold, a plain, scantily-furnished room opened before me, of a nature between a library and a studio. There was not even a carpet on the polished floor, only a rug, which strange to say was not placed in the centre of the room or even before the fireplace, but on one side, and directly in front of a picture that almost at first blush had attracted my attention as being the only article in the room worth looking at. It was the portrait of a woman, handsome, haughty and alluring; a modern beauty, with eyes of fire burning beneath high piled locks of jetty black-ness, that were only relieved from being too intense by the scarlet hood of an opera cloak, that was drawn over them. "A sister," I thought to myself, "it is too modern for his mother," and I took a step nearer to see if I could trace any likeness in the chiselled features of this disdainful brunette, to the more characteristic ones of the careless gentleman who had stood but a few moments before in my presence. As I did so, I was struck with the distance with which the picture stood out from the wall, and thought to myself that the awkwardness of the framing came near marring the beauty of this otherwise lovely work of art. As for the likeness I was in search of, I found it or thought I did, in the expression of the eyes which were of the same color as Mr. Blake's but more full and passionate; and satisfied that I had exhausted all the picture could tell me, I turned to make what other observations I could, when I was startled by confronting the agitated countenance of Mrs. Daniels who had entered behind me.

"This is Mr. Blake's room," said she with dignity; "no one ever intrudes here but myself, not even the servants."

"I beg pardon," said I, glancing around in vain for the something which had awakened that look of satisfaction in Mr. Gryce's eyes. "I was attracted by the beauty of this picture visible through the half open door and stepped in to favor myself with a nearer view. It is very lovely. A sister of Mr. Blake?"

"No, his cousin;" and she closed the door after us with an emphasis that proclaimed she was anything but pleased.

It was my last effort to obtain information on my own account. In a few moments later Mr. Gryce appeared from below, and a conversation ensued with Mrs. Daniels that absorbed my whole attention.

"You are very anxious, my man here tells me, that this girl should be found?" remarked Mr. Gryce; "so much so that you are willing to defray all the expenses of a search?"

She bowed. "As far as I am able sir; I have a few hundreds in the bank, you are welcome to them. I would not keep a dollar back if I had thousands, but I am poor, and can only promise you what I myself possess; though—" and her cheeks grew flushed and hot with an unnatural agitation—"I believe that thousands would not be lacking if they were found necessary. I—I could almost swear you shall have anything in reason which you require; only the girl must be found and soon."

"Have you thought," proceeded Mr. Gryce, utterly ignoring the wildness of these statements, "that the girl may come back herself if let alone?"

"She will come back if she can," quoth Mrs. Daniels.

"Did she seem so well satisfied with her home as to warrant you in saying that?"

"She liked her home, but she loved me," returned the woman steadily. "She loved me so well she would never have gone as she did without being forced. Yes," said she, "though she made no outcry and stopped to put on her bonnet and shawl. She was not a girl to make a fuss. If they had killed her outright, she would never have uttered a cry."

"Why do you say they?"

"Because I am confident I heard more than one man's voice in her room."

"Humph! Would you know those voices if you heard them again?"

"No."

There was a surprise in this last negative which Mr. Gryce evidently noticed.

"I ask," said he, "because I have been told that Mr. Blake lately kept a body servant who has been seen to look at this girl more than once, when she has passed him on the stairs."

Mrs. Daniels' face turned scarlet with rage and she hastily rose from the chair. "I don't believe it," said she; "Henry was a man who knew his place, and—I won't hear such things," she suddenly exclaimed; "Emily was—was a lady, and—"

"Well, well," interposed Mr. Gryce soothingly, "though the cat looks at the king, it is no sign the king looks at the cat. We have to think of everything you know."

"You must never think of anything like that."

Mr. Gryce softly ran his thumb around the brim of the hat he held in his hand. "Mrs. Daniels," observed he, "it would greatly facilitate matters if you would kindly tell us why you take such an interest in this girl. One glimpse at her real history would do more towards setting us on the right track than anything else you could offer."

Her face assumed an unmistakable frown. "Have I not told you," said she, "what is known of it? That she came to me about two years ago for work; that I liked her, and so hired her; that she has been with us ever since and—"

"Then you will not tell us?" exclaimed Mr. Gryce.

Her face fell and a look of hesitation crossed it.

"I doubt if we can do anything unless you do," continued he.

Her countenance settled again into a resolved expression.

"You are mistaken," said she; "if the girl had a secret—as nearly all girls have, brought low as she has evidently been—it had nothing to do with her disappearance, nor would a knowledge of it help you in any way. I am confident of this and so shall hold my peace."

She was not a woman to be frightened or cajoled into making revelations she did not think necessary, and seeing it, Mr. Gryce refrained from urging her further.

"However, you will at least tell me this," said he, "what were the knick-knacks she took away with her from her bureau drawer?"

"No," said she, "for they have nothing to do with her abduction. They were articles of positive value to her, though I assure you of little importance to any one else. All that is shown by their disappearance is the fact that she had a moment's time allowed her in which to collect what she most wanted."

Mr. Gryce arose. "Well," said he, "you have given us a hard sum to work out, but I am not the man to recoil from anything hard. If I can discover the whereabouts of this girl I will certainly do it, but you must help me."

"I, how?"

"By inserting a personal in the Herald. You say she loves you; and would come back if she could. Now whether you believe it or not this is open to doubt; therefore I would advise that you take some such means as that to inform her of the anxiety of her friends and their desire to communicate with her."

"Impossible," she cried vehemently. "I should be afraid—"

"Well?"

"I might put it that Mrs. D——, anxious about Emily, desires information of her whereabouts—"

"Put it any way you like."

"You had better add," said I, speaking for the first time, "that you would be willing to pay for information."

"Yes," said Mr. Gryce, "add that."

Mrs. Daniels frowned, but made no objection, and after getting as minute a description as possible of the clothing worn by the girl the night before, we left the house.

CHAPTER IV.

THOMPSON'S STORY

"An affair of some mystery," remarked Mr. Gryce, as we halted at the corner to take a final look at the house and its environs. "Why a girl should choose such a method of descent as that,"—and he pointed to the ladder down which we believed her to have come—"to leave a house of which she had been an inmate for a year, baffles me, I can tell you. If it were not for those marks of blood which betray her track, I would be disinclined to believe any such hare-brained adventure was ever perpetrated by a woman. As it is, what would'nt I give for her photograph. Black hair, black eyes, white face and thin figure! what a description whereby to find a girl in this great city of New York. Ah!" said he with sudden gratification, "here is Mr. Blake again; his appointment must have been a failure. Let us see if his description will be any more definite." And hurrying towards the advancing figure of that gentleman, he put some questions to him.

Instantly Mr. Blake stopped, looked at him blankly for a moment, then replied in a tone sufficiently loud for me to hear:

"I am sorry, sir, if my description could have done you any good, but I have not the remotest idea how the girl looked. I did not know till this morning even, that there was such a person in my house as a sewing-woman. I leave all such domestic concerns entirely with Mrs. Daniels."

Mr. Gryce again bowed low and ventured another question. The answer came as before, distinctly to my ears.

"O, I may have seen her, I can not say about that; I very often run across the servants in the hall; but whether she is tall or short, light or dark, pretty or ugly, I know no more than you do, sir." Then with a dignified nod calculated to abash a man in Mr. Gryce's position, inquired,

"Is that all?"

It did not seem to be, Mr. Gryce put another question.

Mr. Blake give him a surprised stare before replying, then courteously remarked,

"I do not concern myself with servants after they have left me. Henry was an excellent valet, but a trifle domineering, something which I never allow in any one who approaches me. I dismissed him and that was the end of it, I know nothing of what has become of him."

Mr. Gryce bowed and drew back, and Mr. Blake, with the haughty step peculiar to him, passed by him and reentered his house.

"I should not like to get into that man's clutches," said I, as my superior rejoined me; "he has a way of making one appear so small."

Mr. Gryce shot an askance look at his shadow gloomily following him along the pavement. "Yet it may happen that you will have to run the risk of that very experience."

I glanced towards him in amazement.

"If the girl does not turn up of her own accord, or if we do not succeed in getting some trace of her movements, I shall be tempted to place you where you can study into the ways of this gentleman's household. If the affair is a mystery, it has its centre in that house."

I stared at Mr. Gryce good and roundly. "You have come across something which I have missed," observed I, "or you could not speak so positively."

"I have come across nothing that was not in plain sight of any body who had eyes to see it," he returned shortly.

I shook my head slightly mortified.

"You had it all before you," continued he, "and if you were not able to pick up sufficient facts on which to base a conclusion, you mustn't blame me for it."

More nettled than I would be willing to confess, I walked back with him to the station, saying nothing then, but inwardly determined to reestablish my reputation with Mr. Gryce before the affair was over. Accordingly hunting up the man who had patrolled the district the night before, I inquired if he had seen any one go in or out of the side gate of Mr. Blake's house on — —- street, between the hours of eleven and one.

"No," said he, "but I heard Thompson tell a curious story this morning about some one he had seen."

"What was it?"

"He said he was passing that way last night about twelve o'clock when he remarked standing under the lamp on the corner of Second Avenue, a group consisting of two men and a woman, who no sooner beheld him than they separated, the men drawing back into Second Avenue and the woman coming hastily towards him. Not understanding the move, he stood waiting her approach, when instead of advancing to where he was, she paused at the gate of Mr. Blake's house and lifted her hand as if to open it, when with a wild and terrified gesture she started back, covering her face with her hands, and before he knew it, had actually fled in the direction from which she had come. A little startled, Thompson advanced and looked through the gate before him to see if possible what had alarmed her, when to his great surprise, he beheld the pale face of the master of the house, Mr. Blake himself, looking through the bars from the other side of the gate. He in his turn started back and before he could recover himself, Mr. Blake had disappeared. He says he tried the gate after that, but found it locked."

"Thompson tells you this story, does he?"

"Yes."

"Well," said I, "it's a pretty wild kind of a tale, and all I have got to say is, that neither you nor Thompson had better go blabbing it around too much. Mum is the word where such men as Mr. Blake are concerned." And I departed to hunt up Thompson.

But he had nothing to add to his statement, except that the girl appeared to be tall and thin, and was closely wrapped about in a shawl. My next move was to make such inquiries as I could with safety into the private concerns of Mr. Blake and his family, and discovered—well, such facts as these:

That Mr. Blake was a man who if he paid but little attention to domestic affairs was yet rarely seen out of his own house, except upon occasions of great political importance, when he was always to be found on the platform at meetings of his constituents. Though to the ordinary observer a man eminently calculated, from his good looks, fine position, and solid wealth to enjoy society, he not only manifested a distaste for it, but even went so far as to refuse to participate in the social dinners of his most intimate friends; the only table to which he would sit down being that of some public caterer, where he was sure of finding none but his political associates assembled.

To all appearance he wished to avoid the ladies, a theory borne out by the fact that never, even in church, on the street, or at any place of amusement, was he observed with one at his side. This fact in a man, young—he was not far from thirty-five at that time—rich, and marriageable, would, however, have been more noteworthy than it was if he had not been known to belong to a family eminent for their eccentricities. Not a man of all his race but had possessed some marked peculiarity. His father, bibliomaniac though he was, would never treat a man or a woman with decency, who mentioned Shakspeare to him, nor would he acknowledge to his dying day any excellence in that divine poet beyond a happy way of putting words together. Mr. Blake's uncle hated all members of the legal profession, and as for his grandfather—but you have heard what a mania of dislike he had against that simple article of diet, fish; how his friends were obliged to omit it from their bills of fare whenever they expected him to dinner. If then Mr. Blake chose to have any pet antipathy—as for women for instance—he surely had precedent enough in his own family to back him. However, it was whispered in my ear by one gentleman, a former political colleague of his who had been with him in Washington, that he was known at one time to show considerable attention to Miss Evelyn Blake, that cousin of his who has since made such a brilliant thing of it by marrying, and straightway losing by death, a wealthy old scapegrace of a French noble, the Count De Mirac. But that was not a matter to be talked about, Madame the Countess being free at present and in New York, though to all appearance upon anything but pleasant terms with her quondam admirer.

Remembering the picture I had seen in Mr. Blake's private apartment, I asked if this lady was a brunette, and being told she was, and of the most pronounced type, felt for the moment I had stumbled upon something in the shape of a clue;

but upon resorting to Mr. Gryce with my information, he shook his head with a short laugh and told me I would have to dive deeper than that if I wanted to fish up the truth lying at the bottom of this well.

CHAPTER V.

A NEW YORK BELLE

Meanwhile all our efforts to obtain information in regard to the fate or where-abouts of the missing girl, had so far proved utterly futile. Even the advertisements inserted by Mrs. Daniels had produced no effect; and frustrated in my scheme I began to despair, when the accounts of that same Mrs. Daniels' strange and un-accountable behavior during these days of suspense, which came to me through Fanny, (the pretty housemaid at Mr. Blake's, whose acquaintance I had lately tak-en to cultivating,) aroused once more my dormant energies and led me to ask myself if the affair was quite as hopeless as it seemed.

"If she was a ghost," was her final expression on the subject, "she could'nt go peramberlating this house more than she does. It seems as if she could'nt keep still a minute. Upstairs and down, upstairs and down, till we're most wild. And so white as she is and so trembling! Why her hands shake so all the time she never dares lift a dish off the table. And then the way she hangs about Mr. Blake's door when he's at home! She never goes in, that's the oddest part of it, but walks up and down before it, wringing her hands and talking to herself just like a mad woman. Why, I have seen her almost put her hand on the knob twice in an afternoon per-haps, then draw back as if she was afraid it would burn her; and if by any chance the door opened and Mr. Blake came out, you ought to have seen how she run. What it all means I don't know, but I have my imaginings, and if she is'nt crazy, why—" etc., etc.

In face of facts like these I felt it would be pure insanity to despair. Let there be but a mystery, though it involved a man of the position of Mr. Blake and I was safe. My only apprehension had been that the whole affair would dissolve itself into an ordinary elopement or some such common-place matter.

When, therefore, a few minutes later, Fanny announced that Mr. Blake had ordered a carriage to take him to the Charity Ball that evening, I determined to follow him and learn if possible what change had taken place in himself or his circumstances, to lead him into such an innovation upon his usual habits. Though the hour was late I had but little difficulty in carrying out my plan, arriving at the Academy something less than an hour after the opening dance.

The crowd was great and I circulated the floor three times before I came upon him. When I did, I own I was slightly disappointed; for instead of finding him as I anticipated, the centre of an admiring circle of ladies and gentlemen, I espied him withdrawn into a corner with a bland old politician of the Fifteenth Ward, discussing, as I presently overheard, the merits and demerits of a certain Smith who at that time was making some disturbance in the party.

"If that is all he has come for," thought I, "I had better have stayed at home and made love to the pretty Fanny." And somewhat chagrined, I took up my stand near by, and began scrutinizing the ladies.

Suddenly I felt my heart stand still, the noise of voices ceasing the same instant behind me. A lady was passing on the arm of a foreign-looking gentleman, whom it did not require a second glance to identify with the subject of the portrait in Mr. Blake's house. Older by some few years than when her picture was painted, her beauty had assumed a certain defiant expression that sufficiently betrayed the fact that the years had not been so wholly happy as she had probably anticipated when she jilted handsome Holman Blake for the old French Count. At all events so I interpreted the look of latent scorn that burned in her dark eyes, as she slowly turned her richly bejeweled head towards the corner where that gentleman stood, and meeting his eyes no doubt, bowed with a sudden loss of self-possession that not all the haughty carriage of her noble form, held doubly erect for the next few moments, could quite conceal or make forgotten.

"She still loves him," I inwardly commented and turned to see if the surprise had awakened any expression on his uncommunicative countenance.

Evidently not, for the tough old politician of the Fifteenth Ward was laughing, at one of his own jokes probably, and looking up in the face of Mr. Blake, whose back was turned to me, in a way that entirely precluded all thought of any tragic expression in that quarter. Somewhat disgusted, I withdrew and followed the lady.

I could not get very near. By this time the presence of a live countess in the assembly had become known, and I found her surrounded by a swarm of half-fledged youths. But I cared little for this; all I wanted to know was whether Mr. Blake would approach her or not during the evening. Tediously the moments passed; but a detective on duty, or on fancied duty, succumbs to no weariness. I had a woman before me worth studying and the time could not be thrown away. I learned to know her beauty; the poise of her head, the flush of her cheek, the curl of her lip, the glance—yes, the glance of her eye, though that was more difficult to understand, for she had a way of drooping her lids at times that, while exceedingly effective upon the poor wretch toward whom she might be directing that half-veiled shaft of light, was anything but conducive to my purposes.

At length with a restless shrug of her haughty shoulders she turned away from her crowd of adorers, her breast heaving under its robing of garnet velvet, and her whole face flaring with a light that might mean resolve and might mean simply love. I had no need to turn my head to see who was advancing towards her; her stately attitude as countess, her thrilling glance as woman, betrayed only too readily.

He was the more composed of the two. Bowing over her hand with a few words I could not hear, he drew back a step and began uttering the usual common-place sentiments of the occasion.

She did not respond. With a splendor of indifference not often seen even in the manner of our grandest ladies, she waited, opening and shutting her richly feathered fan, as one who would say, "I know all this has to be gone through with, therefore I will be patient." But as the moments passed, and his tone remained unchanged, I could detect a slight gleam of impatience flash in the depths of her dark eyes, and a change come into the conventional smile that had hitherto lighted, without illuminating her countenance. Drawing still further back from the crowd that was not to be awed from pressing upon her, she looked around as if seeking a refuge. Her glance fell upon a certain window, with a gleam of satisfaction. Seeing they would straightway withdraw there, I took advantage of the moment and made haste to conceal myself behind a curtain as near that vicinity as possible. In another instant I heard them approaching.

"You seem to be rather overwhelmed with attention to-night," were the first words I caught, uttered in Mr. Blake's calmest and most courteous tones.

"Do you think so?" was the slightly sarcastic reply. "I was just deciding to the contrary when you came up."

There was a pause. Taking out my knife, I ripped open a seam in the curtain hanging before me, and looked through. He was eyeing her intently, a firm look upon his face that made its reserve more marked than common. I saw him gaze at her handsome head piled with its midnight tresses amid which the jewels, doubtless of her dead lord, burned with a fierce and ominous glare, at her smooth olive brow, her partly veiled eyes where the fire passionately blazed, at her scarlet lips trembling with an emotion her rapidly flushing cheeks would not allow her to conceal. I saw his glances fall and embrace her whole elegant form with its casing of ruby velvet and ornamentation of lace and diamonds, and an expectant thrill passed through me almost as if I already beheld the mask of his reserve falling, and the true man flash out in response to the wooing beauty of this full-blown rose, evidently in waiting for him. But it died away and a deeper feeling seized me as I saw his glances return unkindled to her countenance, and heard him say in still more measured accents than before:

"Is it possible then that the Countess De Mirac can desire the adulation of us poor American plebeians? I had not thought it, madame."

Slowly her dark eyes turned towards him; she stood a statue.

"But I forget," he went on, a tinge of bitterness for a moment showing itself in his smile: "perhaps in returning to her own country, Evelyn Blake has so far forgotten the last two years as to find pleasure again in the toys and foibles of her youth. Such things have been, I hear." And he bowed almost to the ground in his half sarcastic homage.

"Evelyn Blake! It is long since I have heard that name," she murmured.

He could not restrain the quick flush from mounting to his brow. "Pardon me," said he, "if it brings you sadness or unwelcome memories. I promise you I will not so transgress again."

A wan smile crossed her lips grown suddenly pallid.

"You mistake," said she; "if my name brings up a past laden with bitter memories and shadowed by regret, it also recalls much that is pleasant and never to be forgotten. I do not object to hearing my girlhood's name uttered—by my nearest relative."

The answer was dignity itself. "Your name is Countess De Mirac, your relatives must be proud to utter it."

A gleam not unlike the lightning's quick flash shot from the eyes she drooped before him.

"Is it Holman Blake I am listening to," said she; "I do not recognize my old friend in the cool and sarcastic man of the world now before me."

"We often fail to recognize the work of our hands, madame, after it has fallen from our grasp."

"What," she cried, "do you mean—would you say that—"

"I would say nothing," interrupted he calmly, stooping for the fan she had dropped. "At an interview which is at once a meeting and a parting, I would give utterance to nothing which would seem like recrimination. I—"

"Wait," suddenly exclaimed she, reaching out her hand for her fan with a gesture lofty as it was resolute. "You have spoken a word which demands explanation; what have I ever done to you that you should speak the word recrimination to me?"

"What? You shook my faith in womankind; you showed me that a woman who had once told a man she loved him, could so far forget that love as to marry one she could never respect, for the sake of titles and jewels. You showed me—"

"Hold," said she again, this time without gesture or any movement, save that of her lips grown pallid as marble, "and what did you show me?"

He started, colored profoundly, and for a moment stood before her unmasked of his stern self-possession. "I beg your pardon," said he, "I take back that word, recrimination."

It was now her turn to lift her head and survey him. With glance less cool than his, but fully as deliberate, she looked at his proud head bending before her; studying his face, line by line, from the stern brow to the closely compressed lips on which melancholy seemed to have set its everlasting seal, and a change passed over her countenance. "Holman," said she, with a sudden rush of tenderness, "if in the times gone by, we both behaved with too much worldly prudence for it now to be any great pleasure for either of us to look back, is that any reason why we should mar our whole future by dwelling too long upon what we are surely still young enough to bury if not forget? I acknowledge that I would have behaved in a more ideal fashion, if, after I had been forsaken by you, I had turned my face from society, and let the canker-worm of despair slowly destroy whatever life and bloom I had left. But I was young, and society had its charms, so did the prospect of wealth and position, however hollow they may have proved; you who are the master of both this day, because twelve months ago you forsook Evelyn Blake, should be the last to reproach me with them. I do not reproach you; I only say let the past be forgotten—"

"Impossible," exclaimed he, his whole face darkening with an expression I could not fathom. "What was done at that time cannot be undone. For you and me there is no future. Yes," he said turning towards her as she made a slight fluttering move of dissent, "no future; we can bury the past, but we can not resurrect it. I doubt if you would wish to if we could; as we cannot, of course you will not desire even to converse upon the subject again. Evelyn I wanted to see you once, but I do not wish to see you again; will you pardon my plain speaking, and release me?"

"I will pardon your plain speaking, but—" Her look said she would not release him.

He seemed to understand it so, and smiled, but very bitterly. In another moment he had bowed and gone, and she had returned to her crowd of adoring sycophants.

CHAPTER VI.
A BIT OF CALICO

It was about this time that I took up my residence in a sort of lodging-house that occupied the opposite corner to that of Mr. Blake. My room, as I took pains to have it, overlooked the avenue, and from its windows I could easily watch the goings and comings of the gentleman whose movements were daily becoming of more and more interest to me. For set it down to caprice—and men are often as capricious as women—or account for it as you will, his restlessness at this period was truly remarkable. Not a day that he did not spend his time in walking the streets, and that not in his usual aimless gentlemanly fashion, but eagerly and with an intent gaze that roamed here and there, like a bird seeking its prey. It would often be as late as five o'clock before he came in, and if, as now frequently happened, he did not have company to dinner, he was even known to start out again after seven o'clock and go over the same ground as in the morning, looking with strained gaze, that vainly endeavored to appear unconcerned, into the faces of the women that he passed. I not unfrequently followed him at these times as much for my own amusement as from any hope I had of coming upon anything that should aid me in the work before me. But when he suddenly changed his route of travel from a promenade in the fashionable thoroughfares of Broadway and Fourteenth Street to a walk through Chatham Square and the dark, narrow streets of the East side, I began to scent whom the prey might be that he was seeking, and putting every other consideration aside, regularly set myself to dog his steps, as only I, with my innumerable disguises, knew how to do. For three separate days I kept at his heels wherever he went, each day growing more and more astonished if not to say hopeful, as I found myself treading the narrowest and most disreputable streets of the city; halting at the shops of pawnbrokers; peering into the back-rooms of liquor shops; mixing with the crowds that infest the corner groceries at nightfall, and even slinking with hand on the trigger of the pistol I carried in my pocket, up dark alleys where every door that swung noiselessly to and fro as we passed, shut upon haunts of such villainy as only is known to us of the police, or to those good souls that for the sake of One whose example they follow, lay aside their fears and sensitiveness to carry light into the dim pits of this wretched world. At first I thought Mr. Blake might have some such reason for the peculiar course he took. But his indifference to all crowds where only men were collected, his silence where a word would have been well received, convinced me it was a woman he was seeking and that with an intentness which blinded him to the commonest needs of the hour. I even saw him once in his hurry and abstraction, step across the body of a child who had fallen face downward on the stones, and that with an expression showing he was utterly unconscious of anything but an obstacle in his path. The strangest part of it all was that he seemed to have no fear. To be sure he took pains to leave his watch at home; but with such a figure and carriage as he possessed, the absence of jewelry could never deceive the eye for a moment as to the fact of his being a man of wealth, and those he went among would do anything for money. Perhaps, like me, he carried a pistol. At all events he shunned no spot where either poverty lay hid or deviltry reigned, his proud stern head bending to enter the lowest doors without a tremble of the haughty lips that remained compressed as by an iron force; except when some poor forlorn creature with flaunting head-gear, and tremulous hands, attracted by his bearing would hastily brush against him, when he would turn and look, perhaps speak, though what he said I always failed to catch; after which he would hurry on as if possessed by seven devils. The evenings of those three days were notable also. Two of them he spent in the manner I have described; the third he went to the Windsor House—where the Countess De Mirac had taken rooms—going up to the ladies' entrance and actually ringing the bell, only to start back and walk up and down on the opposite side of the way, with his hands behind his back, and his head bent, evidently deliberating as to whether he should or should not carry out his original intention of entering. The arrival of a carriage with the stately subject of his deliberations, who from her elaborate costume had seemingly been to some kettledrum or private reception, speedily put an end to his doubts. As the door opened to admit her, I saw him cast one look at her heavily draped person, with its snowy opera-cloak drawn tightly over the sweeping folds of her maize colored silk, and shrink back with what sounded like a sigh of anger or distrust, and without waiting for the closing of the door upon her, turn toward home with a step that hesitated no longer.

The fourth day to my infinite chagrin, I was sick and could not go with him. All I could do was to wrap myself in blankets and sit in my window from which I had the satisfaction of viewing him start as I supposed upon his usual course. The rest of the day was employed in a long, dull waiting for his return, only relieved by casual glimpses of Mrs. Daniels' troubled face as she appeared at one window or another of the old-fashioned mansion before me. She seemed, too, to be unusually restless, opening the windows and looking out with forlorn cranings of her neck as if she too were watching for her master. Indeed I have no doubt from what I afterwards learned, that she was in a state of constant suspense during these days. Her frequent appearance at the station house, where she in vain sought for some news of the girl in whose fate she was so absorbed, confirmed this. Only the day before I gave myself up to my unreserved espionage of Mr. Blake, she had had an interview with Mr. Gryce in which she had let fall her apprehensions that the girl was dead, and asked whether if that were the case, the police would be likely to come into a knowledge of the fact. Upon being assured that if she had not been privately made way with, there was every chance in their favor, she had grown a little calmer, but before going away had so far forgotten herself as to intimate that if some result was not reached before another fortnight had elapsed, she should take the matter into her own hands and—She did not say what she would do, but her looks were of a very menacing character. It was no wonder, then, that her countenance bore marks of the keenest anxiety as she trod the halls of that dim old mansion, with its dusky corners rich with bronzes and the glimmering shine of ancient brocades, breathing suggestions of loss and wrong; or bent her wrinkled forehead to gaze from the windows for the coming of one whose footsteps were ever delayed. She happened to be looking out, when after a longer stroll than usual the master of the house returned. As he made his appearance at the corner, I saw her hurriedly withdraw her head and hide herself behind the curtain, from which position she watched him as with tired steps and somewhat dejected mien, he passed up the steps and entered the house. Not till the door closed upon him, did she venture to issue forth and with a hurried movement shut the blinds and disappear. This anxiety on her part redoubled mine, and thankful enough was I when on the next day I found myself well enough to renew my operations. To ferret out this mystery, if mystery it was,—I still found myself forced to admit the possibility of there being none—had now become the one ambition of my life; and all because it was not only an unusually blind one, but of a nature that involved danger to my position as detective, I entered upon it with a zest rare even to me who love my work and all it involves with an undivided passion.

To equip myself, then, in a fresh disguise and to join Mr. Blake shortly after he had left his own corner, was anything but a hardship to me that bright winter morning, though I knew from past experience, a long and wearisome walk was before me with nothing in all probability at the end but reiterated disappointment. But for once the fates had willed it otherwise. Whether Mr. Blake, discouraged at the failure of his own attempts, whatever they were, felt less heart to prosecute them than usual I cannot say, but we had scarcely entered upon the lower end of the Bowery, before he suddenly turned with a look of disgust, and gazing hurriedly about him, hailed a Madison Avenue car that was rapidly approaching. I was at that moment on the other side of the way, but I hurried forward too, and signaled the same car. But just as I was on the point of entering it I perceived Mr. Blake step hastily back and with his eyes upon a girl that was hurrying past him with a basket on her arm, regain the sidewalk with a swiftness that argued his desire to stop her. Of course I let the car pass me, though I did not dare approach him too closely after my late conspicuous attempt to enter it with him. But from my stand on the opposite curb-stone I saw him draw aside the girl, who from her garments might have been the daughter or wife of any one of the shiftless, drinking wretches lounging about on the four corners within my view, and after talking earnestly with her for a few moments, saunter at her side down Broome Street, still talking. Reckless at this sight of the consequences which might follow his detection of the part I was playing, I hasted after them, when I was suddenly disconcerted by observing him hurriedly separate from the girl and turn towards me with intention as it were to regain the corner he had left. Weighing in an instant the probable good to be obtained by following either party, I determined to leave Mr. Blake for one day to himself, and turn my attention to the girl he had addressed, especially as she was tall and thin and bore herself with something like grace.

Barely bestowing a glance upon him, then, as he passed, in a vain attempt to read the sombre expression of his inscrutable face grown five years older in the last five days, I shuffled after the girl now flitting before me down Broome Street. As I did so, I noticed her dress to its minutest details, somewhat surprised to find how ragged and uncouth it was. That Mr. Blake should stop a girl wherever seen, clad in a black alpaca frock, a striped shawl and a Bowery hat trimmed with feathers, I could easily understand; but that this creature with her faded calico dress, dingy cape thrown carelessly over her head, and ragged basket, should arrest his attention, was a riddle to me. I hastened forward with intent to catch a glimpse of her countenance if possible; but she seemed to have acquired wings to her feet since her interview with Mr. Blake. Darting into a crowd of hooting urchins that were rushing from Centre Street after a broken wagon and runaway horse, she sped from my sight with such rapidity, I soon saw that my only hope of overtaking her lay in running. I accordingly quickened my steps when those same hooting youngsters getting in the way of my feet, I tripped up and—well, I own I retired from that field baffled. Not entirely so, however. Just as I was going down, I caught sight of the girl tearing away from a box of garbage on the curb-stone; and when order having been restored, by which lofty statement I mean to say when your humble servant had regained his equilibrium, I awoke to the fact that she had effectually disappeared, I hurried to that box and succeeded in finding hanging to it a bit of rag easily recognized as a piece of the old calico frock of nameless color which I had been following a moment before. Regarding it as the sole spoils of a very unsatisfactory day's work, I put it carefully away in my pocket book, where it lay till—But with all my zeal for compression, I must not anticipate.

When I came home that afternoon I found myself unexpectedly involved in a matter that for the remainder of the day at least, prevented me from further attending to the affair I had in hand. The next morning Mr. Blake did not start out as usual, and at noon I received intimation from Fanny that he was preparing to take a journey. Where, she could not inform me, nor when, though she thought it probable he would take an early train. Mrs. Daniels was feeling dreadfully, she informed me; and the house was like a grave. Greatly excited at this unexpected move on Mr. Blake's part, I went home and packed my valise with something of the spirit of her who once said, under somewhat different circumstances I allow, "Whither thou goest I will go."

The truth was, I had travelled so far and learned so little, that my professional pride was piqued. That expression of Mr. Gryce still rankled, and nothing could soothe my injured spirit now but success. Accordingly when Mr. Blake stepped up to the ticket office of the Hudson River Railroad next morning, to buy a ticket for Putney, a small town in the northern part of Vermont, he found beside him a spruce young drummer, or what certainly appeared such, who by some strange coincidence, wanted a ticket for the same place. The fact did not seem in the least to surprise him, nor did he cast me a look beyond the ordinary glance of one stranger at another. Indeed Mr. Blake had no appearance of being a suspicious man, nor do I think at this time, he had the remotest idea that he was either watched or followed; an ignorance of the truth which I took care to preserve by taking my seat in a different car from him and not showing myself again during the whole ride from New York to Putney.

CHAPTER VII.

THE HOUSE AT THE GRANBY CROSS ROADS

Why Mr. Blake should take a journey at all at this time, and why of all places in the world he should choose such an insignificant town as Putney for his destination, was of course the mystery upon which I brooded during the entire distance. But when somewhere near five in the afternoon I stepped from the cars on to the platform at Putney Station only to hear Mr. Blake making inquiries in regard to a certain stage running between that town and a still smaller village further east, I own I was not only surprised but well-nigh nonplussed. Especially as he seemed greatly disappointed to hear that it only ran once a day, and then for an earlier train in the morning.

"You will have to wait till to-morrow I fear," said the ticket agent, "unless the landlord of the hotel down yonder, can harness you up a team. There is a funeral out west to-day and—"

I did not wait to hear more but hurried down to the hotel he had pointed out, and hunting up the landlord inquired if for love or money he could get me any sort of a conveyance for Melville that afternoon. He assured me it would be impossible, the livery stable as well as his own being entirely empty.

"Such a thing don't happen here once in five years," said he to me. "But the old codger who is dead, though a queer dick was a noted personage in these parts, and not a man, woman or child, who could find a horse, mule or donkey, but what availed himself of the privilege. Even the doctor's spavined mare was pressed into service, though she halts on one leg and stops to get her breath half a dozen times in going up one short hill. You will have to wait for the stage, sir."

"But I am in a hurry," said I as I saw Mr. Blake enter. "I have business in Melville tonight, and I would pay anything in reason to get there."

But the landlord only shook his head; and drawing back with the air of an abused man, I took up my stand in the doorway where I could hear the same colloquy entered into with Mr. Blake, with the same unsatisfactory termination. He did not take it quite as calmly as I did, though he was of too reserved a nature to display much emotion over anything. The prospect of a long tedious evening spent in a country hotel seemed almost unendurable to him, but he finally succumbed to the force of circumstances, as indeed he seemed obliged to do, and partaking of such refreshment as the rather poorly managed hotel afforded, retired without ceremony to his room, from which he did not emerge again till next morning. In all this he had somehow managed not to give his name; and by means of some inquiries I succeeded in making that evening, I found his person was unknown in the town.

By a little management I secured the next room to his, by which arrangement I succeeded in passing a sleepless night, Mr. Blake spending most of the wee sma' hours in pacing the floor of his room, with an unremitting regularity that had anything but a soothing effect upon my nerves. Early the next morning we took the stage, he sitting on the back seat, and I in front with the driver. There were other passengers, but I noticed he never spoke to any of them, nor through all the long drive did he once look up from the corner where he had ensconced himself. It was twelve o'clock when we reached the end of the route, a small town of somewhat less than the usual pretensions of mountain villages; so insignificant indeed, that I found it more and more difficult to imagine what the wealthy ex-Congressman could find in such a spot as this, to make amends for a journey of such length and discomfort; when to my increasing wonder I heard him give orders for a horse to be saddled and brought round to the inn door directly after dinner. This was a move I had not expected and it threw me a little aback, for although I had thus far managed to hold myself so aloof from Mr. Blake, even while keeping him under my eye, that no suspicion of my interest in his movements had as yet been awakened, how could I thus for the third time follow his order with one precisely similar, without attracting an attention that would be fatal to my plans. Yet to let him ride off alone now, would be to drop the trail at the very moment the scent became of importance.

The landlord, a bustling, wiry little man all nervousness and questions, unwittingly helped me at this crisis.

"Are you going on to Perry, sir?" inquired he of that gentleman, "I have been expecting a man along these three days bound for Perry."

"I am that man," I broke in, stepping forward with some appearance of asperity, "and I hope you won't keep me waiting. A horse as soon as dinner is over, do you hear? I am two days late now, and won't stand any nonsense."

And to escape the questions sure to follow, I strode into the dining-room with a half-fierce, half-sullen countenance, that effectually precluded all advances. During the meal I saw Mr. Blake's eye roam more than once towards my face; but I did not return his gaze, or notice him in any way; hurrying through my dinner, and mounting the first horse brought around, as if time were my only consideration. But once on the road I took the first opportunity to draw rein and wait, suddenly remembering that I had not heard Mr. Blake give any intimation of the direction he intended taking. A few minutes revealed to me his elegant form well mounted and showing to perfection in his closely buttoned coat, slowly approaching up the road. Taking advantage of a rise in the ground, I lingered till he was almost upon me, when I cantered quickly on, fearing to arouse his apprehensions if I allowed him to pass me on a road so solitary as that which now stretched out before us: a move provocative of much embarassment to me, as I dared not turn my head for the same reason, anxious as I was to keep him in sight.

The roads dividing before me, at length gave me my first opportunity to pause and look back. He was some fifty paces behind. Waiting till he came up, I bowed with the surly courtesy I thought in keeping with the character I had assumed, and asked if he knew which road led towards Perry, saying I had come off in such haste I had forgotten to inquire my way. He returned my bow, pointed towards the left hand road and saying, "I know this does not," calmly took it.

Now here was a dilemma. If in face of this curt response I proceeded to follow him, my hand was revealed at once; yet the circumstances would admit of no other course. I determined to compromise matters by pretending to take the right hand road till he was out of sight, when I would return and follow him swiftly upon the left. Accordingly I reined my horse to the right, and for some fifteen minutes galloped slowly away towards the north; but another fifteen saw me facing the west, and riding with a force and fury of which I had not thought the old mare they had given me capable, till I put her to the test. It was not long before I saw my fine gentleman trotting in front of me up a long but gentle slope that rose in the distance; and slackening my own rein, I withdrew into the forest at the side of the road, till he had passed its summit and disappeared, when I again galloped forward.

And thus we went on for an hour, over the most uneven country I ever traversed, he always one hill ahead; when suddenly, by what instinct I cannot determine, I felt myself approaching the end, and hastening to the top of the ascent up which I was then laboring, looked down into the shallow valley spread out before me.

What a sight met my eyes if I had been intent on anything less practical than the movements of the solitary horseman below! Hills on hills piled about a verdant basin in whose depths nestled a scanty collection of houses, in number so small they could be told upon the fingers of the right hand, but which notwithstanding lent an indescribable aspect of comfort to this remote region of hill and forest.

But the vision of Mr. Blake pausing half way down the slope before me, examining, yes examining a pistol which he held in his hand, soon put an end to all ideas of romance. Somewhat alarmed I reined back; but his action had evidently no connection with me, for he did not once glance behind him, but kept his eye on the road which I now observed took a short turn towards a house of so weird and ominous an appearance that I scarcely marvelled at his precaution.

Situated on a level track of land at the crossing of three roads, its spacious front, rude and unpainted as it was, presented every appearance of an inn, but from its moss-grown chimneys no smoke arose, nor could I detect any sign of life in its shutterless windows and closed doors, across which shivered the dark shadow of the one gaunt and aged pine, that stood like a guard beside its tumbled-down porch.

Mr. Blake seemed to have been struck by the same fact concerning its loneliness, for hurriedly replacing his pistol in his breast pocket, he rode slowly forward. I instantly conceived the plan of striking across the belt of underbrush that separated me from this old dwelling, and by taking my stand opposite its front, intercept a view of Mr. Blake as he approached. Hastily dismounting, therefore, I led my horse into the bushes and tied her to a tree, proceeding to carry out my plan on foot. I was so far successful as to arrive at the further edge of the wood, which was thick enough to conceal my presence without being too dense to obstruct my vision, just as Mr. Blake passed on his way to this solitary dwelling. He was looking very anxious, but determined. Turning my eyes from him, I took another glance at the house, which by this movement I had brought directly before me. It was even more deserted-looking than I had thought; its unpainted front with its double row of blank windows meeting your gaze without a response, while the huge old pine with half its limbs dismantled of foliage, rattled its old bones against its sides and moaned in its aged fashion like the solitary retainer of a dead race.

I own I felt the cold shivers creep down my back as that creaking sound struck my ears, though as the day was chill with an east wind I dare say it was more the effect of my sudden cessation from exercise, than of any superstitious awe I felt. Mr. Blake seemed to labor under no such impressions. Riding up to the front door he knocked without dismounting, on its dismal panels with his riding whip. No response was heard. Knitting his brows impatiently, he tried the latch: the door was locked. Hastily running his eye over the face of the building, he drew rein and proceeded to ride around the house, which he could easily do owing to the absence of every obstruction in the way of fence or shrubbery. Finding no means of entrance he returned again to the front door which he shook with an impatient hand that however produced no impression upon the trusty lock, and recognizing, doubtless, the futility of his endeavors, he drew back, and merely pausing to give one other look at its deserted front, turned his horse's head, and to my great amazement, proceeded with sombre mien and clouded brow to retake the road to Melville.

This old inn or decayed homestead was then the object of his lengthened and tedious journey; this ancient house rotting away among the bleak hills of Vermont, the bourne towards which his steps had been tending for these past two days. I could not understand it. Rapidly emerging from the spot where I had secreted myself, I in my turn made a circuit of the house, if happily I should discover some loophole of entrance which had escaped his attention. But every door and window was securely barred, and I was about to follow his example and leave the spot, when I saw two or three children advancing towards me down the cross roads, gaily swinging their school books. I noticed they hesitated and huddled together as they approached and saw me, but not heeding this, I accosted them with a pleasant word or so, then pointing over my shoulder to the house behind, asked who lived there. Instantly their already pale faces grew paler.

"Why," cried one, a boy, "don't you know? That is where the two wicked men lived who stole the money out of the Rutland bank. They were put in prison, but they got away and—"

Here, the other, a little girl, plucked him by the sleeve with such affright, that he himself took alarm and just giving me one quick stare out of his wide eyes, grasped his companion by the hand and took to his heels. As for myself I stood rooted to the ground in my astonishment. This blank, sleepy old house the home of the notorious Schoenmakers after whom half of the detectives of the country were searching? I could scarcely credit my own ears. True I now remembered they had come from these parts, still—

Turning round I eyed the house once more. How altered it looked to me! What a murderous aspect it wore, and how dismally secret were the tight shut windows and closely fastened doors, on one of which a rude cross scrawled in red chalk met the eye with a mysterious significance. Even the old pine had acquired the villainous air of the uncanny repositor of secrets too dreadful to reveal, as it groaned and murmured to itself in the keen east wind. Dark deeds and foul wrong seemed written all over the fearful place, from the long strings of black moss that clung to the worm-eaten eaves, to the worn stone with its great blotch of something,— could it have been blood?—that served as a threshold to the door. Suddenly with the quickness of lightning the thought flashed across me, what could Mr. Blake, the aristocratic representative of New York's oldest family, have wanted in this nest of infamy? What errand of hope, fear, despair, avarice or revenge, could have brought this superior gentleman with his refined tastes and proudly reticent manners, so many miles from home, to the forsaken den of a brace of hardy villains whose name for two years now, had stood as the type of all that was bold, bad and lawless, and for whom during the last six weeks the prison had yawned, and the gallows hungered. Contemplation brought no reply, and shocked at my own thoughts, I put the question by for steadier brains than mine; and instead of trying further to solve it, cast about how I was to gain entrance into this deserted building; for to enter it I was more than ever determined, now that I had heard to whom it had once belonged.

Examining with a glance the several roads that branched off in every direction from where I stood, I found them all equally deserted. Even the school children had disappeared in some one of the four or five houses scattered in the remote distance.

If I was willing to enter upon any daring exploit, there was no one to observe or interrupt. I resolved to make the attempt with which my mind was full. This was to climb the old tree, and from one of the two or three branches that brushed against the house, gain entrance at an open garret window that stared at me from amid the pine's dark needles. Taking off my coat with a sigh over the immaculate condition of my new cassimere trousers, I bent my energies to the task. A difficult one you will say for a city lad, but thanks to fortune I was not brought up in New York, and know how to climb trees with the best. With little more than a scratch or so, I reached the window of which I have spoken, and after a moment spent in regaining my breath, gave one spring and accomplished my purpose. I alighted upon a heap of broken glass in a large bare room. An ominous chill at once struck to my heart. Though I am anything but a sensitive man as far as physical impressions are concerned, there was something in the hollow echo that arose from the four blank walls about me as my feet alighted on that rough, uncarpeted floor, that struck a vague chill through my blood, and I actually hesitated for the moment whether to pursue the investigations I had promised myself, or beat a hasty retreat. A glance at the huge distorted limbs swaying across the square of the open window decided me. It was easy to enter by means of that unsteady support, but it would be extremely unsafe to venture forth in that way. If I prized life and limb

I must seek some other method of egress. I at once put my apprehensions in my pocket and entered upon my self imposed task.

A single glance was sufficient to exhaust the resources of the empty garret in which I found myself. Two or three old chairs piled in one corner, a rusty stove or so, a heap of tattered and decaying clothing, were all that met my gaze. Taking my way, then, at once to the ladder, whose narrow ends projecting above a hole in the garret floor, seemed to proffer the means of reaching the rooms below, I proceeded to descend into what to my excited imagination looked like a gulf of darkness. It proved, however, to be nothing more nor less than an unlighted hall of small dimensions, with a stair-case at one end and a door at the other, which, upon opening I found myself in a large, square room whose immense four-post bedstead entirely denuded of its usual accompaniments of bed and bolster at once struck my eye and for a moment held it enchained. There were other articles in the room; a disused bureau, a rocking chair, even a table, but nothing had such a ghostly look as that antique bedstead with its curtains of calico tied back over its naked framework, like rags draped from the bare bones of a skeleton. Passing hurriedly by, I tried a closet door or so, finding little, however, to reward my search; and eager to be done with what was every moment becoming more and more drearisome, I hastened across the floor to the front of the house where I found another hall and a row of rooms that, while not entirely stripped of furniture, were yet sufficiently barren to offer little encouragement to my curiosity. One only, a small but not uncomfortable apartment, showed any signs of having been occupied within a reasonable length of time; and as I paused before its hastily spread bed, thrown together as only a man would do it, and wondering why the room was so dark, looked up and saw that the window was entirely covered by an old shawl and a couple of heavy coats that had been hastily nailed across it, I own I felt my hand go to my breast pocket almost as if I expected to see the wild faces of the dreaded Schoenmakers start up all aglare from one of the dim corners before me. Rushing to the window, I tore down with one sweep of my arm both coat and shawl, and with a start discovered that the window still possessed its draperies in the shape of a pair of discolored and tattered curtains tied with ribbons that must once have been brilliant and cheery of color.

Nor was this the only sign in the room of a bygone presence that had possessed a taste for something beyond the mere necessities of life. On the grim coarsely papered wall hung more than one picture; cut from pictorial newspapers to be sure, but each and every one, if I may be called a judge of such matters, possessing some quality of expression to commend it to a certain order of taste. They were all strong pictures. Vivid faces of men and women in daring positions; a hunter holding back a jaguar from his throat; a soldier protecting his comrade from the stroke; and most striking of all, a woman lissome as she was powerful, starting aghast and horror stricken from—what? I could not tell; a rough hand had stripped the remainder of the picture from the wall.

A bit of candle and a half sheet of a newspaper lay on the floor. I picked up the paper. It was a Rutland Herald and bore the date of two days before. As I read I realized what I had done. If these daring robbers were not at this very moment in the house, they had been there, and that within two or three days. The broken panes of glass in the garret above were now explained. I was not the first one who had climbed that creaking pine tree this fall.

Something like a sensible dread of a very possible danger now seized hold of me. If I had stumbled upon these strangely subtile, yet devilishly bold creatures in their secret lair, the pistol I carried was not going to save me. Shut in like a fox in a hole, I had little to hope for, if they once made their appearance at the stairhead or came upon me from any of the dim halls of the crazy old dwelling, which I now began to find altogether too large for my comfort. Stealing cautiously forth from the room in which I had found so much to disconcert me, I crept towards the front staircase and listened. All was deathly quiet. The old pine tree moaned and twisted without, and from time to time the wind came sweeping down the chimney with an unearthly shrieking sound that was weirdly in keeping with the place. But within and below all was still as the tomb, and though in no ways reassured, I determined to descend and have the suspense over at once. I did so, pistol in hand and ears stretched to their utmost to catch the slightest rustle, but no sound came to disturb me, nor did I meet on this lower floor the sign of any other presence in the house but my own. Passing hastily through what appeared to be a sort of rude parlor, I stepped into the kitchen and tried one of the windows. Finding I could easily lift it from the inside, I drew my breath with ease for the first time since I had alighted among the broken glass above, and turning back, deliberately opened the door of the kitchen stove, and looked in. As I half expected, I found a pile of partly charred rags, showing where the wretches had burned their prison clothing, and proceeding further, picked up from the ashes a ring which whether or not they were conscious of having attempted to destroy in this way I cannot say, but which I thankfully put in my pocket against the day it might be required as proof.

Discerning nothing more in that quarter inviting interest, I asked myself if I had nerve to descend into the cellar. Finally concluding that that was more than could be expected from any man in my position, I gave one look of farewell to the damp and desolate walls about me, then with a breath of relief jumped from the kitchen window again into the light and air of day. As I did so I could swear I heard a door within that old house swing on its hinges and softly close. With a thrill I recognized the fact that it came from the cellar.

* * * * *

My thoughts on the road back to Melville were many and conflicting. Chief above them all, however, rose the comfortable conclusion that in the pursuit of one mysterious affair, I had stumbled, as is often the case, upon the clue to another of yet greater importance, and by so doing got a start that might yet redound greatly to my advantage. For the reward offered for the recapture of the Schoenmakers was large, and the possibility of my being the one to put the authorities upon their track, certainly appeared after this day's developements, open at least to a very reasonable hope. At all events I determined not to let the grass grow under my feet till I had informed the Superintendent of what I had seen and heard that day in the old haunt of these two escaped convicts.

Arrived at the public house in Melville, and learning that Mr. Blake had safely returned there an hour before, I drew the landlord to one side and asked what he could tell me about that old house of the two noted robbers Schoenmaker, I had passed on my way back among the hills.

"Wa'al now," replied he, "this is curious. Here I've just been answering the gentleman up stairs a heap of questions concerning that self same old place, and now you come along with another batch of them; just as if that rickety old den was the only spot of interest we had in these parts."

"Perhaps that may be the truth," I laughed. "Just now when the papers are full of these rogues, anything concerning them must be of superior interest of course." And I pressed him again to give me a history of the house and the two thieves who had inhabited it.

"Wa'al," drawled he "'taint much we know about them, yet after all it may be a trifle too much for their necks some day. Time was when nobody thought especial ill of them beyond a suspicion or so of their being somewhat mean about money. That was when they kept an inn there, but when the robbery of the Rutland bank was so clearly traced to them, more than one man about here started up and said as how they had always suspected them Shoenmakers of being villains, and even hinted at something worse than robbery. But nothing beyond that one rascality has yet been proved against them, and for that they were sent to jail for twenty years as you know. Two months ago they escaped, and that is the last known of them. A precious set, too, they are; the father being only so much the greater rogue than the son as he is years older."

"And the inn? When was that closed?"

"Just after their arrest."

"Has'nt it been opened since?"

"Only once when a brace of detectives came up from Troy to investigate, as they called it."

"Who has the key?"

"Ah, that's more than I can tell you."

I dared not ask how my questions differed from those of Mr. Blake, nor indeed touch upon that point in any way. I was chiefly anxious now to return to New York without delay; so paying my bill I thanked the landlord, and without waiting for the stage, remounted my horse and proceeded at once to Putney where I was fortunate enough to catch the evening train. By five o'clock next morning I was in New York where I proceeded to carry out my programme by hastening at once to headquarters and reporting my suspicions regarding the whereabouts of the Schoenmakers. The information was received with interest and I had the satisfaction of seeing two men despatched north that very day with orders to procure the arrest of the two notable villains wherever found.

CHAPTER VIII.

A WORD OVERHEARD

That evening I had a talk with Fanny over the area gate. She came out when she saw me approach, with her eyes staring and her whole form in a flutter.

"O," she cried, "such things as I have heard this day!"

"Well," said I, "what? let me hear too." She put her hand on her heart. "I never was so frightened," whispered she, "I thought I should have fainted right away. To hear that elegant lady use such a word as crime,—"

"What elegant lady?" interrupted I. "Don't begin in the middle of your story, that's a good girl; I want to hear it all."

"Well," said she, calming down a little, "Mrs. Daniels had a visitor to-day, a lady. She was dressed—"

"O, now," interrupted I for the second time, "you can leave that out. Tell me what her name was and let the fol-de-rols go."

"Her name?" exclaimed the girl with some sharpness, "how should I know her name; she did'nt come to see me."

"How did she look then? You saw her I suppose?"

"And was'nt that what I was telling you, when you stopped me. She looked like a queen, that she did; as grand a lady as ever I see, in her velvet dress sweeping over the floor, and her diamonds as big as—"

"Was she a dark woman?" I asked.

"Her hair was black and so were her eyes, if that is what you mean."

"And was she very tall and proud looking?"

The girl nodded. "You know her?" whispered she.

"No," said I, "not exactly; but I think I can tell who she is. And so she called to-day on Mrs. Daniels, did she."

"Yes, but I guess she knew master would be home before she got away."

"Come," said I, "tell me all about it; I'm getting impatient."

"And ain't I telling you?" said she. "It was about three o'clock this afternoon, the time I go up stairs to dress, so I just hangs about in the hall a bit, near the parlor door, and I hear her gossiping with Mrs. Daniels almost as if she was an old friend, and Mrs. Daniels answering her mighty stiffly and as if she was'nt glad to see her at all. But the lady didn't seem to mind, but went on talking as sweet as honey, and when they came out, you would have thought she loved the old woman like a sister to see her look into her face and say something about knowing how busy she was, but that it would give her so much pleasure if she would come some day to see her and talk over old times. But Mrs. Daniels was'nt pleased a bit and showed plain enough she did'nt like the lady, fine as she was in her ways. She was going to answer her too, but just then the front door opened and Mr. Blake with his satchel in his hand, came into the house. And how he did start, to be sure, when he saw them, though he tried to say something perlite which she did'nt seem to take to at all, for after muttering something about not expecting to see him, she put her hand on the knob and was going right out. But he stopped her and they went into the parlor together while Mrs. Daniels stood staring after them like one mad, her hand held out with his bag and umbrella in it, stiff as a statter in the Central Park. She did'nt stand so long, though, but came running down the hall, as if she was bewitched. I was dreadful flustered, for though I was hid behind the wall that juts out there by the back stairs, I was afraid she would see me and shame me before Mr. Blake. But she passed right by and never looked up. 'There is something dreadful mysterious in this,' thought I, and I just made up my mind to stay where I was till Mr. Blake and the lady should come out again from the parlor. I did'nt have to wait very long. In a few minutes the door opened and they stepped out, he ahead and she coming after. I thought this was queer, he is always so dreadful perlite in his ways, but I thought it was a deal queerer when I saw him go up the front stairs, she hurrying after, looking I cannot tell you how, but awful troubled and anxious, I should say.

"They went into that room of his he calls his studio and though I knew it might cost me my place if I was found out, I could'nt help following and listening at the keyhole."

"And what did you hear?" I asked, for she paused to take breath.

"Well, the first thing I heard was a cry of pleasure from her, and the words, 'You keep that always before you? You cannot dislike me, then, as much as you pretend.' I don't know what she meant nor what he did, but he stepped across the room and I heard her cry out this time as if she was hurt as well as awful surprised; and he talked and talked, and I could'nt catch a word, he spoke so low; and by and by she sobbed just a little, and I got scared and would have run away but she cried out with a kind of shriek, 'O, don't say any more; to think that crime should come into our family, the proudest in the land. How could you, Holman, how could you.' Yes," the girl went on, flushing in her excitement till she was as red as the cherry ribbons in her cap, "those were the very words she used: 'To think that crime should come into our family! the proudest one in the land!' And she called him by his first name, and asked him how he could do it."

"And what did Mr. Blake say?" returned I, a little taken back myself at this result of my efforts with Fanny.

"O, I did'nt wait to hear. I did'nt wait for anything. If folks was going to talk about such things as that, I thought I had better be anywhere than listening at the keyhole. I went right up stairs I can tell you."

"And whom have you told of what you heard in the half dozen hours that have gone by?"

"Nobody; how could you think so mean of me when I promised, and—"

It is not necessary to go any further into this portion of the interview.

The Countess De Mirac possessed to its fullest extent the present fine lady's taste for bric-a-brac. So much I had learned in my inquiries concerning her. Remembering this, I took the bold resolution of profiting by this weakness of hers to gain admission to her presence, she being the only one sharing Mr. Blake's mysterious secret. Borrowing a valuable antique from a friend of mine at that time in the business, I made my appearance the very next day at her apartments, and sending in an urgent request to see Madame, by the trim negress who answered my summons, waited in some doubt for her reply.

It came all too soon; Madame was ill and could see no one. I was not, however, to be baffled by one rebuff. Handing the basket I held to the girl, I urged her to take it in and show her mistress what it contained, saying it was a rare article which might never again come her way.

The girl complied, though with a doubtful shake of the head which was anything but encouraging. Her incredulity, however, must have been speedily rebuked, for she almost immediately returned without the basket, saying Madame would see me.

My first thoughts upon entering the grand lady's presence, was that the girl had been mistaken, for I found the Countess walking the floor in an abstracted way, drying a letter she had evidently but just completed, by shaking it to and fro with an unsteady hand; the placque I had brought, lying neglected on the table.

But at sight of my respectful form standing with bent head in the doorway, she hurriedly thrust the letter into a book and took up the placque. As she did so I marked her well and almost started at the change I observed in her since that evening at the Academy. It was not only that she was dressed in some sort of loose dishabille that was in eminent contrast to the sweeping silks and satins in which I had hitherto beheld her adorned; or that she was laboring under some physical disability that robbed her dark cheek of the bloom that was its chiefest charm. The change I observed went deeper than that; it was more as if a light had been extinguished in her countenance. It was the same woman I had beheld standing like a glowing column of will and strength before the melancholy form of Mr. Blake, but with the will and strength gone, and with them all the glow.

"She no longer hopes," thought I, and already felt repaid for my trouble.

"This is a very pretty article you have brought me," said she with something of the unrestrained love of art which she undoubtedly possessed, showing itself through all her languor. "Where did it come from, and what recommendations have you, to prove it is an honest sale you offer me?"

"None," returned I, ignoring with a reassuring smile the first question, "except that I should not be afraid if all the police in New York knew I was here with this fine placque for sale."

She gave a shrug of her proud shoulder that bespoke the French Countess and softly ran her finger round the edge of the placque.

"I don't need anything more of this kind," said she languidly; "besides," and she set it down with a fretful air, "I am in no mood to buy this afternoon." Then shortly, "What do you ask for it?"

I named a fabulous price.

She started and cast me a keen glance. "You had better take it to some one else; I have no money to throw away."

With a hesitating hand I lifted the placque towards the basket. "I would very much like to sell it to you," said I. "Perhaps—"

Just then a lady's fluttering voice rose from the room beyond inquiring for the Countess, and hurriedly taking the placque from my hand with an impulsive "O there's Amy," she passed into the adjoining apartment, leaving the door open behind her.

I saw a quick interchange of greetings between her and a fashionably dressed lady, then they withdrew to one side with the ornament I had brought, evidently consulting in regard to its merits. Now was my time. The book in which she had placed the letter she had been writing lay on the table right before me, not two inches from my hand. I had only to throw back the cover and my curiosity would be satisfied. Taking advantage of a moment when their backs were both turned, I pressed open the book with a careful hand, and with one eye on them and one on the sheet before me, managed to read these words:—

MY DEAREST CECILIA.

I have tried in vain to match the sample you sent me at Stewart's, Arnold's and McCreery's. If you still insist upon making up the dress in the way you propose, I will see what Madame Dudevant can do for us, though I cannot but advise you to alter your plans and make the darker shade of velvet do. I went to the Cary reception last night and met Lulu Chittenden. She has actually grown old, but was as lively as ever. She created a great stir in Paris when she was there; but a husband who comes home two o'clock in the morning with bleared eyes and empty pockets, is not conducive to the preservation of a woman's beauty. How she manages to retain her spirits I cannot imagine. You ask me news of cousin Holman. I meet him occasionally and he looks well, but has grown into the most sombre man you ever saw. In regard to certain hopes of which you have sometimes made mention, let me assure you they are no longer practicable. He has done what—

Here the conversation ceased in the other room, the Countess made a movement of advance and I closed the book with an inward groan over my ill-luck.

"It is very pretty," said she with a weary air; "but as I remarked before, I am not in the buying mood. If you will take half you mention, I may consider the subject, but—"

"Pardon me, Madame," I interrupted, being in no wise anxious to leave the placque behind me, "I have been considering the matter and I hold to my original price. Mr. Blake of Second Avenue may give it to me if you do not."

"Mr. Blake!" She eyed me suspiciously. "Do you sell to him?"

"I sell to anyone I can," replied I; "and as he has an artist's eye for such things—"

Her brows knitted and she turned away. "I do not want it;" said she, "sell it to whom you please."

I took up the placque and left the room.

CHAPTER IX.

A FEW GOLDEN HAIRS

When a few days from that I made my appearance before Mr. Gryce, it was to find him looking somewhat sober. "Those Schoenmakers," said he, "are making a deal of trouble. It seems they escaped the fellows up north and are now somewhere in this city, but where—"

An expressive gesture finished the sentence.

"Is that so?" exclaimed I. "Then we are sure to nab them. Given time and a pair of low, restless German thieves, I will wager anything, our hands will be upon them before the month is over. I only hope, when we do come across them, it will not be to find their betters too much mixed up with their devilish practices." And I related to him what Fanny had told me a few evenings before.

"The coil is tightening," said he. "What the end will be I don't know. Crime, said she? I wish I knew in what blind hole of the earth that girl we are after lies hidden."

As if in answer to this wish the door opened and one of our men came in with a letter in his hand. "Ha!" exclaimed Mr. Gryce, after he had perused it, "look at that."

I took the letter from his hand and read:

The dead body of a girl such as you describe was found in the East river off Fiftieth Street this morning. From appearance has been dead some time. Have telegraphed to Police Headquarters for orders. Should you wish to see the body before it is removed to the Morgue or otherwise disturbed, please hasten to Pier 48 E. R. GRAHAM.

"Come," said I, "let's go and see for ourselves. If it should be the one—"

"The dinner party proposed by Mr. Blake for to-night, may have its interruptions," he remarked.

I do not wish to make my story any longer than is necessary, but I must say that when in an hour or so later, I stood with Mr. Gryce before the unconscious form of that poor drowned girl I felt an unusual degree of awe stealing over me: there was so much mystery connected with this affair, and the parties implicated were of such standing and repute.

I almost dreaded to see the covering removed from her face lest I should behold, what? I could not have told if I had tried.

"A trim made body enough," cried the official in charge as Mr. Gryce lifted an end of the cloth that enveloped her and threw it back. "Pity the features are not better preserved."

"No need for us to see the features," exclaimed I, pointing to the locks of golden red hair that hung in tangled masses about her. "The hair is enough; she is not the one." And I turned aside, asking myself if it was relief I felt.

To my surprise Mr. Gryce did not follow.

"Tall, thin, white face, black eyes." I heard him whisper to himself. "It is a pity the features are not better preserved."

"But," said I, taking him by the arm, "Fanny spoke particularly of her hair being black, while this girl's—Good heavens!" I suddenly ejaculated as I looked again at the prostrate form before me. "Yellow hair or black, this is the girl I saw him speaking to that day in Broome Street. I remember her clothes if nothing more." And opening my pocketbook, I took out the morsel of cloth I had plucked that day from the ash barrel, lifted up the discolored rags that hung about the body and compared the two. The pattern, texture and color were the same.

"Well," said Mr. Gryce, pointing to certain contusions, like marks from the blow of some heavy instrument on the head and bared arms of the girl before us; "he will have to answer me one question anyhow, and that is, who this poor creature is who lies here the victim of treachery or despair." And turning to the official he asked if there were any other signs of violence on the body.

The answer came deliberately, "Yes, she has evidently been battered to death."

Mr. Gryce's lips closed with grim decision. "A most brutal murder," said he and lifting up the cloth with a hand that visibly trembled, he softly covered her face.

"Well," said I as we slowly paced back up the pier, "there is one thing certain, she is not the one who disappeared from Mr. Blake's house."

"I am not so sure of that."

"How!" said I. "You believed Fanny lied when she gave that description of the missing girl upon which we have gone till now?"

Mr. Gryce smiled, and turning back, beckoned to the official behind us. "Let me have that description," said he, "which I distributed among the Harbor Police some days ago for the identification of a certain corpse I was on the lookout for."

The man opened his coat and drew out a printed paper which at Mr. Gryce's word he put into my hand. It ran as follows:

Look out for the body of a young girl, tall, well shaped but thin, of fair complexion and golden hair of a peculiar bright and beautiful color, and when found, acquaint me at once.

G.

"I don't understand," began I.

But Mr. Gryce tapping me on the arm said in his most deliberate tones, "Next time you examine a room in which anything of a mysterious nature has occurred, look under the bureau and if you find a comb there with several long golden hairs tangled in it, be very sure before you draw any definite conclusions, that your Fannys know what they are talking about when they declare the girl who used that comb had black hair on her head."

CHAPTER X.

THE SECRET OF MR. BLAKE'S STUDIO

"Mr. Blake is at dinner, sir, with company, but I will call him if you say so."

"No," returned Mr. Gryce; "show us into some room where we can be comfortable and we will wait till he has finished."

The servant bowed, and stepping forward down the hall, opened the door of a small and cosy room heavily hung with crimson curtains. "I will let him know that you are here," said he, and vanished towards the dining-room.

"I doubt if Mr. Blake will enjoy the latter half of his bill of fare as much as the first," said I, drawing up one of the luxurious arm-chairs to the side of my principal. "I wonder if he will break away from his guests and come in here?"

"No; if I am not mistaken we shall find Mr. Blake a man of nerve. Not a muscle of his face will show that he is disturbed."

"Well," said I, "I dread it."

Mr. Gryce looked about on the gorgeous walls and the rich old fashioned furniture that surrounded him, and smiled one of his grimmest smiles.

"Well, you may," said he.

The next instant a servant stood in the doorway, bearing to our great astonishment, a tray well set with decanter and glasses.

"Mr. Blake's compliments, gentlemen," said he, setting it down on the table before us. "He hopes you will make yourselves at home and he will see you as soon as possible."

The humph! of Mr. Gryce when the servant had gone would have done your soul good, also the look he cast at the pretty Dresden Shepherdess on the mantel-piece, as I reached out my hand towards the decanter. Somehow it made me draw back.

"I think we had better leave his wine alone," said he.

And for half an hour we sat there, the wine untouched between us, listening alternately to the sound of speech-making and laughter that came from the dining-room, and the solemn ticking of the clock as it counted out the seconds on the mantel-piece. Then the guests came in from the table, filing before us past the open door on their way to the parlors. They were all gentlemen of course—Mr. Blake never invited ladies to his house—and gentlemen of well known repute. The dinner had been given in honor of a certain celebrated statesman, and the character of his guests was in keeping with that of the one thus complimented.

As they went by us gaily indulging in the jokes and light banter with which such men season a social dinner, I saw Mr. Gryce's face grow sober by many a shade; and when in the midst of it all, we heard the voice of Mr. Blake rise in that courteous and measured tone for which it is distinguished, I saw him reach forward and grasp his cane with an uneasiness I had never seen displayed by him before. But when some time later, the guests having departed, the dignified host advanced with some apology to where we were, I never beheld a firmer look on Mr. Gryce's face than that with which he rose and confronted him. Mr. Blake's own had not more character in it.

"You have called at a rather inauspicious time, Mr. Gryce," said the latter, glancing at the card which he held in his hand. "What may your business be? Something to do with politics, I suppose."

I surveyed the man in amazement. Was this great politician stooping to act a part, or had he forgotten our physiognomies as completely as appeared?

"Our business is not politics," replied Mr. Gryce; "but fully as important. May I request the doors be closed?"

I thought Mr. Blake looked surprised, but he immediately stepped to the door and shut it. Then coming back, he looked at Mr. Gryce more closely and a change took place in his manner.

"I think I have seen you before," said he.

Mr. Gryce bowed with just the suspicion of a smile. "I have had the honor of consulting you before in this very house," observed he.

A look of full recognition passed over the dignified countenance of the man before us.

"I remember," said he, shrugging his shoulders in the old way. "You are interested in some servant girl or other who ran away from this house a week or so ago. Have you found her?" This with no apparent concern.

"We think we have," rejoined Mr. Gryce with some solemnity. "The river gives up its prey now and then, Mr. Blake."

Still only that look of natural surprise.

"Indeed! You do not mean to say she has drowned herself? I am sorry for that, a girl who had once lived in my house. What trouble could she have had to drive her to such an act?"

Mr. Gryce advanced a step nearer the gentleman.

"That is what we have come here to learn," said he with a deliberation that yet was not lacking in the respect due to a man so universally esteemed as Mr. Blake. "You who have seen her so lately ought to be able to throw some light upon the subject at least."

"Mr.—" he again glanced at the card, "Mr. Gryce,—excuse me—I believe I told you when you were here before that I had no remembrance of this girl at all. That if such a person was in my house I did not know it, and that all questions put to me on that subject would be so much labor thrown away."

Mr. Gryce bowed. "I remember," said he. "I was not alluding to any connection you may have had with the girl in this house, but to the interview you were seen to have with her on the corner of Broome Street some days ago. You had such an interview, did you not?"

A flush, deep as it was sudden, swept over Mr. Blake's usually unmoved cheek. "You are transgressing sir," said he and stopped. Though a man of intense personal pride, he had but little of that quality called temper, or perhaps if he had, thought it unwise to display it on this occasion. "I saw and spoke to a girl on the corner of that street some days ago," he went on more mildly, "but that she was the one who lived here, I neither knew at the time nor feel willing to believe now without positive proof." Then in a deep ringing tone the stateliness of which it would be impossible to describe, he inquired, "Have the city authorities presumed to put a spy on my movements, that the fact of my speaking to a poor forsaken creature on the corner of the street should be not only noted but remembered?"

"Mr. Blake," observed Mr. Gryce, and I declare I was proud of my superior at that moment, "no man who is a true citizen and a Christian should object to have his steps followed, when by his own thoughtlessness, perhaps, he has incurred a suspicion which demands it."

"And do you mean to say that I have been followed," inquired he, clenching his hand and looking steadily, but with a blanching cheek, first at Mr. Gryce then at me.

"It was indispensable," quoth that functionary gently.

The outraged gentleman riveted his gaze upon me. "In town and out of town?" demanded he.

I let Mr. Gryce reply. "It is known that you have lately sought to visit the Schoenmakers," said he.

Mr. Blake drew a deep breath, cast his eyes about the handsome apartment in which we were, let them rest for a moment upon a portrait that graced one side of the wall, and which was I have since learned a picture of his father, and slowly drew forward a chair. "Let me hear what your suspicions are," said he.

I noticed Mr. Gryce colored at this; he had evidently been met in a different way from what he expected. "Excuse me," said he, "I do not say I have any suspicions; my errand is simply to notify you of the death of the girl you were seen to speak with, and to ask whether or not you can give us any information that can aid us in the matter before the coroner."

"You know I have not. If I have been as closely followed as you say, you must know why I spoke to that girl and others, why I went to the house of the Schoenmakers and—Do you know?" he suddenly inquired.

Mr. Gryce was not the man to answer such a question as that. He eyed the rich signet ring that adorned the hand of the gentleman before him and suavely smiled. "I am ready to listen to any explanations," said he.

Mr. Blake's haughty countenance became almost stern. "You consider you have a right to demand them; let me hear why."

"Well," said Mr. Gryce with a change of tone, "you shall. Unprofessional as it is, I will tell you why I, a member of the police force, dare enter the house of such a man as you are, and put him the questions I have concerning his domestic affairs. Mr. Blake, imagine yourself in a detective's office. A woman comes in, the housekeeper of a respected citizen, and informs us that a girl employed by her as seamstress has disappeared in a very unaccountable way from her master's house the night before; in fact been abducted as she thinks from certain evidences, through the window. Her manner is agitated, her appeal for assistance urgent, though she acknowledges no relationship to the girl or expresses any especial cause for her interest beyond that of common humanity. 'She must be found,' she declares, and hints that any sum necessary will be forthcoming, though from what source after her own pittance is expended she does not state. When asked if her master has no interest in the matter, she changes color and puts us off. He never noticed his servants, left all such concerns to her, etc.; but shows fear when a proposition is made to consult him. Next imagine yourself with the detectives in that gentleman's house. You enter the girl's room; what is the first thing you observe? Why that it is not only one of the best in the house, but that it is conspicuous for its comforts if not for its elegancies. More than that, that there are books of poetry and history lying around, showing that the woman who inhabited it was above her station; a fact which the housekeeper is presently brought to acknowledge. You notice also that the wild surmise of her abduction by means of the window, has some ground in appearance, though the fact that she went with entire unwillingness is not made so apparent. The housekeeper, however, insists in a way that must have had some special knowledge of the girl's character or circumstances to back it, that she never went without compulsion; a statement which the torn curtains and the track of blood over the roof of the extension, would seem to emphasize. A few other facts are made known. First, a pen-knife is picked up from the grass plot in the yard beneath, showing with what instrument the wound was inflicted, whose drippings made those marks of blood alluded to. It was a pearl-handled knife belonging to the writing desk found open on her table, and its frail and dainty character proved indisputably, that it was employed by the girl herself, and that against manifest enemies; no man being likely to snatch up any such puny weapon for the purpose either of offence or defence. That these enemies were two and were both men, was insisted upon by Mrs. Daniels who overheard their voices the night before.

"Mr. Blake, such facts as these arouse curiosity, especially when the master of the house being introduced upon the scene, he fails to manifest common human interest, while his housekeeper betrays in every involuntary gesture and expression she makes use of, her horror if not her fear of his presence, and her relief at his departure. Yes," he exclaimed, unheeding the sudden look here cast him by Mr. Blake, "and curiosity begets inquiry, and inquiry elucidated further facts such as these, that the mysterious master of the house was in his garden at the hour of the girl's departure, was even looking through the bars of his gate when she, having evidently escaped from her captors, came back with every apparent desire to re-enter her home, but seeing him, betrayed an unreasonable amount of fear and fled back even into the very arms of the men she had endeavored to avoid. Did you speak sir?" asked Mr. Gryce suddenly stopping, with a sly look at his left boot tip.

Mr. Blake shook his head. "No," said he shortly, "go on." But that last remark of Mr. Gryce had evidently made its impression.

"Inquiry revealed, also, two or three other interesting facts. First, that this gentleman qualified though he was to shine in ladies' society, never obtruded himself there, but employed his leisure time instead, in walking the lower streets of the city, where he was seen more than once conversing with certain poor girls at street corners and in blind alleys. The last one he talked with, believed from her characteristics to be the same one that was abducted from his house—"

"Hold there," said Mr. Blake with some authority in his tone, "there you are mistaken; that is impossible."

"Ah, and why?"

"The girl you allude to had bright golden hair, something which the woman who lived in my house did not possess."

"Indeed. I thought you had never noticed the woman who sewed for you, sir,—did not know how she looked?"

"I should have noticed her if she had had such hair as the girl you speak of."

Mr. Gryce smiled and opened his pocketbook.

"There is a sample of her hair, sir," said he, taking out a thin strand of brilliant hair and showing it to the gentleman before him. "Bright you see, and golden as that of the unfortunate creature you talked with the other night."

Mr. Blake stooped forward and lifted it with a hand that visibly trembled. "Where did you get this?" asked he at last, clenching it to his breast with sudden passion.

"From out of the comb which the girl had been using the night before."

The imperious man flung it hastily from him.

"We waste our time," said he, looking Mr. Gryce intently in the face. "All that you have said does not account for your presence here nor the tone you have used while addressing me. What are you keeping back? I am not a man to be trifled with."

Mr. Gryce rose to his feet. "You are right," said he, and he gave a short glance in my direction. "All that I have said would not perhaps justify me in this intrusion, if—" he looked again towards me. "Do you wish me to continue?" he asked.

Mr. Blake's intent look deepened. "I see no reason why you should not utter the whole," said he. "A good story loses nothing by being told to the end. You wish to say something about my journey to Schoenmaker's house, I suppose."

Mr. Gryce gravely shook his head.

"What, you can let such a mystery as that go without a word?"

"I am not here to discuss mysteries that have no connection with the sewing-girl in whose cause I am interested."

"Then," said Mr. Blake, turning for the first time upon my superior with all the dignified composure for which he was eminent, "it is no longer necessary for us to prolong this interview. I have allowed, nay encouraged you to state in the plainest terms what it was you had or imagined you had against me, knowing that my actions of late, seen by those who did not possess the key to them, must have seemed a little peculiar. But when you say you have no interest in any mystery disconnected with the girl who has lived the last few months in my house, I can with assurance say that it is time we quitted this unprofitable conversation, as nothing which I have lately done, said or thought here or elsewhere has in any way had even the remotest bearing upon that individual; she having been a stranger to me while in my house, and quite forgotten by me, after her unaccountable departure hence."

Mr. Gryce's hand which had been stretched out towards the hitherto untouched decanter before him, suddenly dropped. "You deny then," said he, "all connection between yourself and the woman, lady or sewing-girl, who occupied that room above our heads for eleven months previous to the Sunday morning I first had the honor to make your acquaintance."

"I am not in the habit of repeating my assertions," said Mr. Blake with some severity, "even when they relate to a less disagreeable matter than the one under discussion."

Mr. Gryce bowed, and slowly reached out for his hat; I had never seen him so disturbed. "I am sorry," he began and stopped, fingering his hat-brim nervously. Suddenly he laid his hat back, and drew up his form into as near a semblance of dignity as its portliness would allow.

"Mr. Blake," said he, "I have too much respect for the man I believed you to be when I entered this house to-night, to go with the thing unsaid which is lying at present like a dead weight upon my lips. I dare not leave you to the consequence of my silence; for duty will compel me to speak some day and in some presence where you may not have the opportunity which you can have here, to explain yourself with satisfaction. Mr. Blake I cannot believe you when you say the girl who lived in this house was a stranger to you."

Mr. Blake drew his proud form up in a disdain that was only held in check by the very evident honesty of the man before him. "You are courageous at least," said he. "I regret you are not equally discriminating." And raising Mr. Gryce's hat he placed it in his hand.

"Pardon me," said that gentleman, "I would like to justify myself before I go. Not with words," he proceeded as the other folded his arms with a sarcastic bow. "I am done with words; action accomplishes the rest. Mr. Blake I believe you consider me an honest officer and a reliable man. Will you accompany me to your private room for a moment? There is something there which may convince you I was neither playing the fool nor the bravado when I uttered the phrase I did an instant ago."

I expected to hear the haughty master of the house refuse a request so peculiar. But he only bowed, though in a surprised way that showed his curiosity if no more was aroused. "My room and company are at your disposal," said he, "but you will find nothing there to justify you in your assertions."

"Let me at least make the effort," entreated my superior.

Mr. Blake smiling bitterly immediately led the way to the door. "The man may come," he remarked carelessly as Mr. Gryce waved his hand in my direction. "Your justification if not mine may need witnesses."

Rejoiced at the permission, for my curiosity was by this time raised to fever pitch, I at once followed. Not without anxiety. The assured poise of Mr. Blake's head seemed to argue that the confidence betrayed by my superior might receive a shock; and I felt it would be a serious blow to his pride to fail now. But once within the room above, my doubts speedily fled. There was that in Mr. Gryce's face which anyone acquainted with him could not easily mistake. Whatever might be the mysterious something which the room contained, it was evidently sufficient in his eyes to justify his whole conduct.

"Now sir," said Mr. Blake, turning upon my superior with his sternest expression, "the room and its contents are before you; what have you to say for yourself."

Mr. Gryce equally stern, if not equally composed, cast one of his inscrutable glances round the apartment and without a word stepped before the picture that was as I have said, the only ornamentation of the otherwise bare and unattractive room.

I thought Mr. Blake looked surprised, but his face was not one that lightly expressed emotion.

"A portrait of my cousin the Countess De Mirac," said he with a certain dryness of tone hard to interpret.

Mr. Gryce bowed and for a moment stood looking with a strange lack of interest at the proudly brilliant face of the painting before him, then to our great amazement stepped forward and with a quick gesture turned the picture rapidly to the wall, when—Gracious heavens! what a vision started out before us from the reverse side of that painted canvas! No luxurious brunette countenance now, steeped in pride and languor, but a face—Let me see if I can describe it. But no, it was one of those faces that are indescribable. You draw your breath as you view it; you feel as if you had had an electric shock; but as for knowing ten minutes later whether the eyes that so enthralled you were blue or black, or the locks that clustered halo-like about a forehead almost awful in its expression of weird, unfathomable power, were brown or red, you could not nor would you pretend to say. It was the character of the countenance itself that impressed you. You did not even know if this woman who might have been anything wonderful or grand you ever read of, were beautiful or not. You did not care; it was as if you had been gazing on a tranquil evening sky and a lightning flash had suddenly startled you. Is the lightning beautiful? Who asks! But I know from what presently transpired, that the face was ivory pale in complexion, the eyes deeply dark, and the hair, —strange and uncanny combination, —of a bright and peculiar golden hue.

"You dare!" came forth in strange broken tones from Mr. Blake's lips.

I instantly turned towards him. He was gazing with a look that was half indignant, half menacing at the silent detective who with eyes drooped and finger directed towards the picture, seemed to be waiting for him to finish.

"I do not understand an audacity that allows you to—to—" Was this the haughty gentleman we had known, this hesitating troubled man with bloodless lips and trembling hands?

"I declared my desire to justify myself," said my principal with a respectful bow. "This is my justification. Do you note the color of the woman's hair whose portrait hangs with its face turned to the wall in your room? Is it like or unlike that of the strand you held in your hand a few moments ago; a strand taken as I swear, hair by hair from the comb of the poor creature who occupied the room above. But that is not all," he continued as Mr. Blake fell a trifle aback; "just observe the dress in which this woman is painted; blue silk you see, dark and rich; a wide collar cunningly executed, you can almost trace the pattern; a brooch; then the roses in the hand, do you see? Now come with me upstairs."

Too much startled to speak, Mr. Blake, haughty aristocrat as he was, turned like a little child and followed the detective who with an assured step and unembarassed mien led the way into the deserted room above.

"You accuse me of insulting you, when I express disbelief of your assertion that there was no connection between you and the girl Emily," said Mr. Gryce as he lit the gas and unlocked that famous bureau drawer. "Will you do so any longer in face of these?" And drawing off the towel that lay uppermost, he revealed the neatly folded dress, wide collar, brooch and faded roses that lay beneath. "Mrs. Daniels assures us these articles belonged to the sewing-woman Emily; were brought here by her. Dare you say they are not the ones reproduced in the portrait below?"

Mr. Blake uttering a cry sank on his knees before the drawer. "My God! My God!" was his only reply, "what are these?" Suddenly he rose, his whole form quivering, his eyes burning. "Where is Mrs. Daniels?" he cried, hastily advancing and pulling the bell. "I must see her at once. Send the house-keeper here," he ordered as Fanny smiling demurely made her appearance at the door.

"Mrs. Daniels is out," returned the girl, "went out as soon as ever you got up from dinner, sir."

"Gone out at this hour?"

"Yes sir; she goes out very often nowadays, sir."

Her master frowned. "Send her to me as soon as she returns," he commanded, and dismissed the girl.

"I don't know what to make of this," he now said in a strange tone, approaching again the touching contents of that open bureau drawer with a look in which longing and doubt seemed in some way to be strangely commingled. "I cannot explain the presence of these articles in this room; but if you will come below I will see what I can do to make other matters intelligible to you. Disagreeable as it is for me to take anyone into my confidence, affairs have gone too far for me to hope any longer to preserve secrecy as to my private concerns."

CHAPTER XI.

LUTTRA

"Gentlemen," said he as he ushered us once more into his studio, "you have presumed, and not without reason I should say, to infer that the original of this portrait and the woman who has so long occupied the position of sewing-woman in my house, are one and the same. You will no longer retain that opinion when I inform you that this picture, strange as it may appear to you, is the likeness of my wife."

"Wife!" We both were astonished as I take it, but it was my voice which spoke. "We were ignorant you ever had a wife."

"No doubt," continued our host smiling bitterly, "that at least has evaded the knowledge even of the detectives." Then with a return to his naturally courteous manner, "She was never acknowledged by me as my wife, nor have we ever lived together, but if priestly benediction can make a man and woman one, that woman as you see her there is my lawful wife."

Rising, he softly turned the lovely, potent face back to the wall, leaving us once more confronted by the dark and glowing countenance of his cousin.

"I am not called upon," said he, "to go any further with you than this. I have told you what no man till this hour has ever heard from my lips, and it should serve to exonerate me from any unjust suspicions you may have entertained. But to one of my temperament, secret scandal and the gossip it engenders is only less painful than open notoriety. If I leave the subject here, a thousand conjectures will at once seize upon you, and my name if not hers will become, before I know it, the football of gossip if not of worse and deeper suspicion than has yet assailed me. Gentleman I take you to be honest men; husbands, perhaps, and fathers; proud, too, in your way and jealous of your own reputation and that of those with whom you are connected. If I succeed in convincing you that my movements of late have been totally disconnected with the girl whose cause you profess solely to be interested in, may I count upon your silence as regards those actions and the real motive that led to them?"

"You may count upon my discretion as regards all matters that do not come under the scope of police duty," returned Mr. Gryce. "I haven't much time for gossip."

"And your man here?"

"O, he's safe where it profits him to be."

"Very well, then, I shall count upon you."

And with the knitted brows and clinched hands of a proudly reticent man who, perhaps for the first time in his life finds himself forced to reveal his inner nature to the world, he began his story in these words:

"Difficult as it is for me to introduce into a relation like this the name of my father, I shall be obliged to do so in order to make my conduct at a momentous crisis of my life intelligible to you. My father, then, was a man of strong will and a few but determined prejudices. Resolved that I should sustain the reputation of the family for wealth and respectability, he gave me to understand from my earliest years, that as long as I preserved my manhood from reproach, I had only to make my wishes known, to have them immediately gratified; while if I crossed his will either by indulging in dissipation or engaging in pursuits unworthy of my name, I no longer need expect the favor of his countenance or the assistance of his purse.

"When, therefore, at a certain period of my life, I found that the charms of my cousin Evelyn were making rather too strong an impression upon my fancy for a secured peace of mind, I first inquired how such a union would affect my father, and learning that it would be in direct opposition to his views, cast about in my mind what I should do to overcome my passion. Travel suggested itself, and I took a trip to Europe. But the sight of new faces only awakened in me comparisons anything but detrimental to the beauty of her who was at that time my standard of feminine loveliness. Nature and the sports connected with a wild life were my next resort. I went overland to California, roamed the orange groves of Florida, and probed the wildernesses of Canada and our Northern states. It was during these last excursions that an event occurred which has exercised the most material influence upon my fate, though at the time it seemed to me no more than the matter of a day.

"I had just returned from Canada and was resting in tolerable enjoyment of a very beautiful autumn at Lake George, when a letter reached me from a friend then loitering in the vicinity, urging me to join him in a certain small town in Vermont where trout streams abounded and what is not so often the case under the circumstances, fishers were few.

"Being in a somewhat reckless mood I at once wrote a consent, and before another day was over, started for the remote village whence his letter was postmarked. I found it by no means easy of access. Situated in the midst of hills some twenty miles or so distant from any railroad, I discovered that in order to reach it, a long ride in a stage-coach was necessary, followed by a somewhat shorter journey on horseback. Not being acquainted with the route, I timed my connections wrong, so that when evening came I found myself riding over a strange road in the darkest night I had ever known. As if this was not enough, my horse suddenly began to limp and presently became so lame I found it impossible to urge her beyond a slow walk. It was therefore with no ordinary satisfaction that I presently beheld a lighted building in the distance, which as I approached resolved itself into an inn. Stopping in front of the house, which was closed against the chill night air, I called out lustily for someone to take my horse, whereupon the door opened and a man appeared on the threshold with a lantern in his hand. I at once made my wishes known, receiving in turn a somewhat gruff,

"'Well it is a nasty night and it will be nastier before it's over;' an opinion instantly endorsed by a sudden swoop of wind that rushed by at that moment, slamming the door behind him and awakening over my head a lugubrious groaning as from the twisting boughs of some old tree, that was almost threatening in its character.

"'You had better go in,' said he, 'the rain will come next.'

"I at once leaped from my horse and pushing open the door with main strength, entered the house. Another man met me on the threshold who merely pointing over his shoulder to a lighted room in his rear, passed out without a word, to help the somewhat younger man, who had first appeared, in putting up my horse. I at once accepted his silent invitation and stepped into the room before me. Instantly I found myself confronted by the rather startling vision of a young girl of a unique and haunting style of beauty, who rising at my approach now stood with her eyes on my face and her hands resting on the deal table before which she had been sitting, in an attitude expressive of mingled surprise and alarm. To see a woman in that place was not so strange; but such a woman! Even in the first casual glance I gave her, I at once acknowledged to myself her extraordinary power. Not the slightness of her form, the palor of her countenance, or the fairness of the locks of golden red hair that fell in two long braids over her bosom, could for a moment counteract the effect of her dark glance or the vivid almost unearthly force of her expression. It was as if you saw a flame upstarting before you, waving tremulously here and there, but burning and resistless in its white heat. I took off my hat with deference.

"A shudder passed over her, but she made no effort to return my acknowledgement. As we cast our eyes dilating with horror, down some horrible pit upon whose verge we suddenly find ourselves, she allowed her gaze for a moment to dwell upon my face, then with a sudden lifting of her hand, pointed towards the door as if to bid me depart—when it swung open with that shrill rushing of wind that involuntarily awakes a shudder within you, and the two men entered and came stamping up to my side. Instantly her hand sunk, not feebly as with fear, but calmly as if at the bidding of her will, and without waiting for them to speak, she turned away and quietly left the room. As the door closed upon her I noticed that she wore a calico frock and that her face did not own one perfect feature.

"'Go after Luttra and tell her to make up the bed in the northwest room,' said the elder of the two in deep gutteral tones unmistakably German in their accent, to the other who stood shaking the wet off his coat into the leaping flames of a small wood fire that burned on the hearth before us.

"'O, she'll do without my bothering,' was the sullen return. 'I'm wet through.'

"The elder man, a large powerfully framed fellow of some fifty years or so, frowned. It was an evil frown, and the younger one seemed to feel it. He immediately tossed his coat onto a chair and left the room.

"'Boys are so obstropolous now-a-days,' remarked his companion to me with what he evidently intended for a conciliatory nod. 'In my time they were broke in, did what they were told and asked no questions.'

"I smiled to myself at his calling the broad shouldered six-footer who had just left us a boy, but merely remarking, 'He is your son is he not!' seated myself before the blaze which shot up a tongue of white flame at my approach, that irresistibly recalled to my fancy the appearance of the girl who had gone out a moment before.

"'O, yes, he is my son, and that girl you saw here was my daughter; I keep this inn and they help me, but it is a slow way to live, I can tell you. Travel on these roads is slim.'

"'I should think likely,' I returned, remembering the half dozen or so hills up which I had clambered since I took to my horse. 'How far are we from Pentonville?'

"'O, two or three miles,' he replied, but in a hurried kind of a way. 'Not far in the daytime but a regular journey in a night like this?'

"'Yes,' said I, as the house shook under a fresh gust; 'it is fortunate I have a place in which to put up.'

"He glanced down at my baggage which consisted of a small hand bag, an over-coat and a fishing pole, with something like a gleam of disappointment.

"'Going fishing?' he asked.

"'Yes,' I returned.

"'Good trout up those streams and plenty of them,' he went on. 'Going alone?'

"I did not half like his importunity, but considering I had nothing better to do, replied as affably as possible. 'No, I expect to meet a friend in Pentonville who will accompany me."

"His hand went to his beard in a thoughtful attitude and he cast me what, with my increased experience of the world, I should now consider a sinister glance. 'Then you are expected?' said he.

"Not considering this worth reply, I stretched out my feet to the blaze and began to warm them, for I felt chilled through.

"'Been on the road long?' he now asked, glancing at the blue flannel suit I wore.

"'All summer,' I returned,

"I again thought he looked disappointed.

"'From Troy or New York?' he went on with a vague endeavor to appear good naturally off hand.

"'New York.'

"'A big place that,' he continued. 'I was there once, lots of money stored away in them big buildings down in Wall Street, eh?'

"I assented, and he drew a chair up to my side, a proceeding that was interrupted, however, by the reentrance of his son, who without any apology crowded into the other side of the fire-place in a way to sandwich me between them. Not fancying this arrangement which I, however, imputed to ignorance, I drew back and asked if my room was ready. It seemed it was not, and unpleasantly as it promised, I felt forced to reseat myself and join in, if not support, the conversation that followed.

"A half hour passed away, during which the wind increased till it almost amounted to a gale. Spurts of rain dashed against the windows with a sharp crackling sound that suggested hail, while ever and anon a distant roll as of rousing thunder, rumbled away among the hills in a long and reverberating peal, that made me feel glad to be housed even under the roof of these rude and uncongenial creatures. Suddenly the conversation turned upon the time and time-pieces, when in a low even tone I heard murmured behind me,

"'The gentleman's room is ready;' and turning, I saw standing in the doorway the slight figure of the young girl whose appearance had previously so impressed me.

"I immediately arose. 'Then I will proceed to it at once,' said I, taking up my traps and advancing towards her.

"'Do not be alarmed if you hear creaks and cracklings all over the house,' observed the landlord as I departed. 'The windows are loose and the doors ill-fitting. In such a storm as this they make noise enough to keep an army awake. The house is safe enough though and if you don't mind noise—'

"'O I don't mind noise,' rejoined I, feeling at that moment tired enough to fall into a doze on the staircase. 'I shall sleep, never fear,' and without further ado followed the girl upstairs into a large clumsily furnished room whose enormous bed draped with heavy curtains at once attracted my attention.

"'O I cannot sleep under those things,' remarked I, with a gesture towards the dismal draperies which to me were another name for suffocation.

"With a single arm-sweep she threw them back. 'Is there anything more I can do for you?' asked she, glancing hastily about the room.

"I thanked her and said 'no,' at which she at once departed with a look of still determination upon her countenance that I found it hard to explain.

"Left alone in that large, bare and dimly lighted room, with the wind shrieking in the chimney and the powerful limbs of some huge tree beating against the walls without, with a heavy thud inexpressibly mournful, I found to my surprise and something like dismay, that the sleepiness which had hitherto oppressed me, had in some unaccountable way entirely fled. In vain I contemplated the bed, comfortable enough now in its appearance that the stifling curtains were withdrawn; no temptation to invade it came to arouse me from the chair into which I had thrown myself. It was as if I felt myself under the spell of some invisible influence that like the eye of a basilisk, held me enchained. I remember turning my head towards a certain quarter of the wall as if I half expected to encounter there the bewildering glance of a serpent. Yet far from being apprehensive of any danger, I only wondered over the weakness of mind that made such fancies possible.

"An extra loud swirl of the foliage without, accompanied by a quick vibration of the house, aroused me at last. If I was to lose the sense of this furious storm careering over my head, I must court sleep at once. Rising, I drew off my coat, unloosened my vest and was about to throw it off, when I bethought me of a certain wallet it contained. Going to the door in some unconscious impulse of precaution I suppose, I locked myself in, and then drawing out my wallet, took from it a roll of bills which I put into a small side pocket, returning the wallet to its old place.

"Why I did this I can scarcely say. As I have before intimated, I was under no special apprehension. I was at that time anything but a suspicious man, and the manner and appearance of the men below struck me as unpleasantly disagreeable but nothing more. But I not only did what I have related, but allowed the lamp to remain lighted, lying down finally in my clothes; an almost unprecedented act on my part, warranted however as I said to myself, by the fury of the gale which at that time seemed as if it would tumble the roof over our heads.

"How long I lay listening to the creakings and groanings of the rickety old house, I cannot say, nor how long I remained in the doze which finally seized me as I became accustomed to the sounds around and over me. Enough that before the storm had passed its height, I awoke as if at the touch of a hand, and leaping with a bound out of the bed, beheld to my incredible amazement, the alert, nervous form of Luttra standing before me. She had my coat in her hand, and it was her touch that had evidently awakened me.

"'I want you to put this on,' said she in a low thrilling tone totally new in my experience, 'and come with me. The house is unsafe for you to remain in. Hear how it cracks and trembles. Another blast like that and we shall be roofless.'

"She was moving toward the door, which to my amazement stood ajar, but my hesitation stopped her.

"'Won't you come?' she whispered, turning her face towards me with a look of such potent determination, I followed in spite of myself 'I dare not let you stay here, your blood will be upon my head.'

"'You exaggerate,' I replied, shrinking back with a longing look at the comfortable bed I had just left. 'These old houses are always strong. It will take many such a gust as that you hear, to overturn it, I assure you.'

"'I exaggerate!' she returned with a look of scorn impossible to describe. 'Hark!' she said, 'hear that.'

"I did hear, and I must acknowledge that it seemed is if we were about to be swept from our foundations.

"'Yes,' said I, 'but it is a fearful night to be out in.'

"'I shall go with you,' said she.

"'In that case—' I began with an ill-advised attempt at gallantry which she cut short with a gesture.

"'Here is your hat,' remarked she, 'and here is your bag. The fishing-pole must remain, you cannot carry it.'

"'But,—' I expostulated.

"'Hush!' said she with her ear turned towards the depths of the staircase at the top of which we stood. 'My father and brother will think as you do that it is folly to leave the shelter of a roof for the uncertainties of the road on such a night as this, but you must not heed them. I tell you shelter this night is danger, and that the only safety to be found is on the stormy highway.'

"And without waiting for my reply, she passed rapidly down stairs, pushed open a door at the bottom, and stepped at once into the room we had left an hour or so before.

"What was there in that room that for the first time struck an ominous chill as of distinct peril through my veins? Nothing at first sight, everything at the second. The fire which had not been allowed to die out, still burned brightly on the ruddy hearthstone, but it was not that which awakened my apprehension. Nor was it the loud ticking clock on the mantel-piece with its hand pointing silently to the hour of eleven. Nor yet the heavy quiet of the scantily-furnished room with its one lamp burning on the deal table against the side of the wall. It was the sight of those two powerful men drawn up in grim silence, the one against the door leading to the front hall, the other against that opening into the kitchen.

"A glance at Luttra standing silent and undismayed at my side, however, instantly reassured me. With that will exercised in my favor, I could not but win through whatever it was that menaced me. Slinging my bag over my shoulder, I made a move towards the door and the silent figure of my host. But with a quick outreaching of her hand, she drew me back.

"'Stand still!' said she. 'Karl,' she went on, turning her face towards the more sullen but less intent countenance of her brother, 'open the door and let this gentleman pass. He finds the house unsafe in such a gale and desires to leave it. At once!' she continued as her brother settled himself more determinedly against the lock: 'I don't often ask favors.'

"'The man is a fool that wants to go out in a night like this,' quoth the fellow with a dogged move; 'and so are you to encourage it. I think too much of your health to allow it.'

"She did not seem to hear. 'Will you open the door?' she went on, not advancing a step from the fire, before which she had placed herself and me.'

"'No, I won't,' was the brutal reply. 'Its been locked for the night and its not me nor one like me, that will open it.'

"With a sudden whitening of her already pale face, she turned towards her father. He was not even looking at her.

"'Some one must open the house,' said she, glancing back at her brother. 'This gentleman purposes to leave and his whim must be humored. Will you unlock that door or shall I?'

"An angry snarl interrupted her. Her father had bounded from the door where he stood and was striding hastily towards her. In my apprehension I put up my arm for a shield, for he looked ready to murder her, but I let it drop again as I caught her glance which was like white flame undisturbed by the least breeze of personal terror.

"'You will stop there,' said she, pointing to a spot a few feet from where she stood. 'Another step and I let that for which I have heard you declare you would peril your very soul, fall into the heart of the flames.' And drawing from her breast a roll of bills, she stretched them out above the fire before which she was standing.

"'You — —-' broke from the gray-bearded lips of the old man, but he stopped where he was, eyeing those bills as if fascinated.

"'I am not a girl of many words, as you know,' continued she in a lofty tone inexpressibly commanding. 'You may strangle me, you may kill me, it matters little; but this gentleman leaves the house this night, or I destroy the money with a gesture.'

"'You — —-' again broke from those quivering lips, but the old man did not move.

"Not so the younger. With a rush he left his post and in another instant would have had his powerful arms about her slender form, only that I met him half way with a blow that laid him on the floor at her feet. She said nothing, but one of the bills immediately left her hand and fluttered into the fire where it instantly shrivelled into nothing.

"With the yell of a mad beast wounded in his most vulnerable spot, the old man before us stamped with his heel upon the floor.

"'Stop!' cried he; and going rapidly to the front door he opened it. 'There!' shrieked he, 'if you will be fools, go! and may the lightning blast you. But first give me the money.'

"'Come from the door,' said she, reaching out her left hand for the lantern hanging at the side of the fireplace, 'and let Karl light this and keep himself out of the way.'

"It was all done. In less time than I can tell it, the old man had stepped from the door, the younger one had lit the lantern and we were in readiness to depart.

"'Now do you proceed,' said she to me, 'I will follow.'

"'No,' said I, 'we will go together.'

"'But the money?' growled the heavy voice of my host over my shoulder.

"'I will give it to you on my return,' said the girl."

CHAPTER XII.

A WOMAN'S LOVE

"Shall I ever forget the blast of driving rain that struck our faces and enveloped us in a cloud of wet, as the door swung on its hinges and let us forth into the night; or the electric thrill that shot through me as that slender girl grasped my hand and drew me away through the blinding darkness. It was not that I was so much affected by her beauty as influenced by her power and energy. The fury of the gale seemed to bend to her will, the wind lend wings to her feet. I began to realize what intellect was. Arrived at the roadside, she paused and looked back. The two burly forms of the men we had left behind us were standing in the door of the inn; in another moment they had plunged forth and towards us. With a low cry the young girl leaped towards a tree where to my unbounded astonishment I beheld my horse standing ready saddled. Dragging the mare from her fastenings, she hung the lantern, burning as it was, on the pommel of the saddle, struck the panting creature a smart blow upon the flank, and drew back with a leap to my side.

"The startled horse snorted, gave a plunge of dismay and started away from us down the road.

"'We will wait,' said Luttra.

"The words were no sooner out of her mouth than her father and brother rushed by.

"'They will follow the light,' whispered she; and seizing me again by the hand, she hurried me away in the direction opposite to that which the horse had taken. 'If you will trust me, I will bring you to shelter,' she murmured, bending her slight form to the gusty wind but relaxing not a whit of her speed.

"'You are too kind,' I murmured in return. 'Why should you expose yourself to such an extent for a stranger?'

"Her hand tightened on mine, but she did not reply, and we hastened on as speedily as the wind and rain would allow. After a short but determined breasting of the storm, during which my breath had nearly failed me, she suddenly stopped.

"'Do you know,' she exclaimed in a low impressive tone, 'that we are on the verge of a steep and dreadful precipice? It runs along here for a quarter of a mile and it is not an uncommon thing for a horse and rider to be dashed over it in a night like this.'

"There was something in her manner that awakened a chill in my veins almost as if she had pointed out some dreadful doom which I had unwittingly escaped.

"'This is, then, a dangerous road,' I murmured.

"'Very,' was her hurried and almost incoherent reply.

"How far we travelled through the mud and tangled grasses of that horrible road I do not know. It seemed a long distance; it was probably not more than three quarters of a mile. At last she paused with a short 'Here we are;' and looking up, I saw that we were in front of a small unlighted cottage.

"No refuge ever appeared more welcome to a pair of sinking wanderers I am sure. Wet to the skin, bedrabbled with mud, exhausted with breasting the gale, we stood for a moment under the porch to regain our breath, then with her characteristic energy she lifted the knocker and struck a smart blow on the door.

"'We will find shelter here,' said she.

"She was not mistaken. In a few moments we were standing once more before a comfortable fire hastily built by the worthy couple whose slumbers we had thus interrupted. As I began to realize the sweetness of conscious safety, all that this young, heroic creature had done for me swept warmly across my mind. Looking up from the fire that was beginning to infuse its heat through my grateful system, I surveyed her as she slowly undid her long braids and shook them dry over the blaze, and almost started to see how young she was. Not more than sixteen I should say, and yet what an invincible will shone from her dark eyes and dignified her slender form; a will gentle as it was strong, elevated as it was unbending. I bowed my head as I watched her, in grateful thankfulness which I presently put into words.

"At once she drew herself erect. 'I did but my duty,' said she quietly. 'I am glad I was prospered in it.' Then slowly. 'If you are grateful, sir, will you promise to say nothing of—of what took place at the inn?'

"Instantly I remembered a suspicion which had crossed my mind while there, and my hand went involuntarily to my vest pocket. The roll of bills was gone.

"She did not falter. 'I would be relieved if you would,' continued she.

"I drew out my empty hand, looked at it, but said nothing.

"'Have you lost anything?' asked she. 'Search in your overcoat pockets.'

"I plunged my hand into the one nearest her and drew it out with satisfaction; the roll of bills was there. 'I give you my promise,' said I.

"'You will find a bill missing,' she murmured; 'for what amount I do not know; the sacrifice of something was inevitable.'

"'I can only wonder over the ingenuity you displayed, as well as express my appreciation for your bravery,' returned I with enthusiasm. 'You are a noble girl.'

"She put out her hand as if compliments hurt her. 'It is the first time they have ever attempted anything like that,' cried she in a quick low tone full of shame and suffering. 'They have shown a disposition to—to take money sometimes, but they never threatened life before. And they did threaten yours. They saw you take out your money, through a hole pierced in the wall of the room you occupied, and the sight made them mad. They were going to kill you and then tumble you and your horse over the precipice below there. But I overheard them talking and when they went out to saddle the horse, I hurried up to your room to wake you. I had to take possession of the bills; you were not safe while you held them. I took them quietly because I hoped to save you without betraying them. But I failed in that. You must remember they are my father and my brother.'

"'I will not betray them,' said I.

"She smiled. It was a wintry gleam but it ineffably softened her face. I became conscious of a movement of pity towards her.

"'You have a hard lot,' remarked I. 'Your life must be a sad one.'

"She flashed upon me one glance of her dark eye. 'I was born for hardship,' said she, 'but—' and a sudden wild shudder seized her, 'but not for crime.'

"The word fell like a drop of blood wrung from her heart.

"'Good heavens!' cried I, 'and must you—'

"'No,' rang from her lips in a clarion-like peal; 'some things cut the very bonds of nature. I am not called upon to cleave to what will drag me into infamy.' Then calmly, as if speaking of the most ordinary matter in the world, 'I shall never go back to that house we have left behind us, sir.'

"'But,' cried I, glancing at her scanty garments, 'where will you go? What will you do? You are young—'

"'And very strong,' she interrupted. 'Do not fear for me.' And her smile was like a burst of sudden sunshine.

"I said no more that night.

"But when in the morning I stumbled upon her sitting in the kitchen reading a book not only above her position but beyond her years, a sudden impulse seized me and I asked her if she would like to be educated. The instantaneous illumining of her whole face was sufficient reply without her low emphatic words,

"'I would be content to study on my knees to know what some women do, whom I have seen.'

"It is not necessary for me to relate with what pleasure I caught at the idea that here was a chance to repay in some slight measure the inestimable favor she had done me; nor by what arguments I finally won her to accept an education at my hands as some sort of recompense for the life she had saved. The advantage which it would give her in her struggle with the world she seemed duly to appreciate, but that so great a favor could be shown her without causing me much trouble and an unwarrantable expense, she could not at once be brought to comprehend, and till she could, she held out with that gentle but inflexible will of hers. The battle, however, was won at last and I left her in that little cottage, with the understanding that as soon as the matter could be arranged, she was to enter a certain boarding-school in Troy with the mistress of which I was acquainted. Meanwhile she was to go out to service at Melville and earn enough money to provide herself with clothes.

"I was a careless fellow in those days but I kept my promise to that girl. I not only entered her into that school for a course of three years, but acting through its mistress who had taken a great fancy to her, supplied her with the necessities her position required. It was so easy; merely the signing of a check from time to time, and it was done. I say this because I really think if it had involved any personal sacrifice on my part, even of an hour of my time, or the labor of a thought, I should not have done it. For with my return to the city my interest in my cousin revived, absorbing me to such an extent that any matter disconnected with her soon lost all charm for me.

"Two years passed; I was the slave of Evelyn Blake, but there was no engagement between us. My father's determined opposition was enough to prevent that. But there was an understanding which I fondly hoped would one day open for me the way of happiness. But I did not know my father. Sick as he was—he was at that time laboring under the disease which in a couple of months later bore him to the tomb—he kept an eye upon my movements and seemed to probe my inmost heart. At last he came to a definite decision and spoke.

"His words opened a world of dismay before me. I was his only child, as he remarked, and it had been and was the desire of his heart to leave me as rich and independent a man as himself. But I seemed disposed to commit one of those acts against which he had the most determined prejudice; marriage between cousins being in his eyes an unsanctified and dangerous proceeding, liable to consequences the most unhappy. If I persisted, he must will his property elsewhere. The Blake estate should never descend with the seal of his approbation to a race of probable imbeciles.

"Nor was this enough. He not only robbed me of the woman I loved, but with a clear insight into the future, I presume, insisted upon my marrying some one else of respectability and worth before he died. 'Anyone whose appearance will do you credit and whose virtue is beyond reproach,' said he. 'I don't ask her to be rich or even the offspring of one of our old families. Let her be good and pure and of no connection to us, and I will bless her and you with my dying breath.'

"The idea had seized upon him with great force, and I soon saw he was not to be shaken out of it. To all my objections he returned but the one word,

"'I don't restrict your choice and I give you a month in which to make it. If at the end of that time you cannot bring your bride to my bedside, I must look around for an heir who will not thwart my dying wishes.'"

"A month! I surveyed the fashionable belles that nightly thronged the parlors of my friends and felt my heart sink within me. Take one of them for my wife, loving another woman? Impossible. Women like these demanded something in return for the honor they conferred upon a man by marrying him. Wealth? they had it. Position? that was theirs also. Consideration? ah, what consideration had I to give? I turned from them with distaste.

"My cousin Evelyn gave me no help. She was a proud woman and loved my money and my expectations as much as she did me.

"'If you must marry another woman to retain your wealth, marry, said she, 'but do not marry one of my associates. I will have no rival in my own empire; your wife must be a plainer and a less aspiring woman than Evelyn Blake. Yet do not discredit your name, — which is mine,' she would always add.

"Meanwhile the days flew by. If my own conscience had allowed me to forget the fact, my father's eagerly inquiring, but sternly unrelenting gaze as I came each evening to his bedside, would have kept it sufficiently in my mind. I began to feel like one in the power of some huge crushing machine whose slowly descending weight he in vain endeavors to escape.

"How or when the thought of Luttra first crossed my mind I cannot say. At first I recoiled at the suggestion and put it away from me in disdain; but it ever recurred and with it so many arguments in her favor that before long I found my-self regarding it as a refuge. To be sure she was a waif and a stray, but that seemed to be the kind of wife demanded of me. She was allied to rogues if not villains, I knew; but then had she not cut all connection with them, dropped away from them, planted her feet on new ground which they would never invade? I com-menced to cherish the idea. With this friendless, grateful, unassuming protegee of mine for a wife, I would be as little bound as might be. She would ask nothing, and I need give nothing, beyond a home and the common attentions required of a gentleman and a friend. Then she was not disagreeable, nor was her beauty of a type to suggest the charms of her I had lost. None of the graces of the haughty patrician lady whose lightest gesture was a command, would appear in this hum-ble girl, to mock and constrain me. No, I should have a fair wife and an obedient one, but no vulgarized shadow of Evelyn, thank God, or of any of her fashionably dressed friends.

"Advanced thus far towards the end, I went to see Luttra. I had not beheld her since the morning we parted at the door of that little cottage in Vermont, and her presence caused me a shock. This, the humble waif with the appealing grateful eyes I had expected to encounter? this tall and slender creature with an aureola of golden hair about a face that it was an education to behold! I felt a half movement of anger as I surveyed her. I had been cheated; I had planted a grape seed and a palm tree had sprung up in its place. I was so taken aback, my salute lost some-thing of the benevolent condescension I had intended to infuse into it. She seemed to feel my embarassment and a half smile fluttered to her lips. That smile decided me. It was sweet but above all else it was appealing.

"How I won that woman to marry me in ten days time I care not to state. Not by holding up my wealth and position before her. Something restrained me from that. I was resolved, and perhaps it was the only point of light in my conduct at that time, not to buy this young girl. I never spoke of my expectations, I never al-luded to my present advantages yet I won her.

"We were married, there, in Troy in the quietest and most unpretending man-ner. Why the fact has never transpired I cannot say. I certainly took no especial pains to conceal it at the time, though I acknowledge that after our separation I did resort to such measures as I thought necessary, to suppress what had become gall and wormwood to my pride.

"My first move after the ceremony was to bring her immediately to New York and to this house. With perhaps a pardonable bitterness of spirit, I had refrained from any notification of my intentions, and it was as strangers might enter an unprepared dwelling, that we stepped across the threshold of this house and passed immediately to my father's room.

"'I can give you no wedding and no honeymoon,' I had told her. 'My father is dying and demands my care. From the altar to a death-bed may be sad for you, but it is an inevitable condition of your marriage with me.' And she had accepted her fate with a deep unspeakable smile it has taken me long months of loneliness and suffering to understand.

"'Father, I bring you my bride,' were my first words to him as the door closed behind us shutting us in with the dread, invisible Presence that for so long a time had been relentlessly advancing upon our home.

"I shall never forget how he roused himself in his bed, nor with what eager eyes he read her young face and surveyed her slight form swaying towards him in her sudden emotion like a flame in a breeze. Nor while I live shall I lose sight of the spasm of uncontrollable joy with which he lifted his aged arms towards her, nor the look with which she sprang from my side and nestled, yes nestled, on the breast that never to my remembrance had opened itself to me even in the years of my earliest childhood. For my father was a stern man who believed in holding love at arm's length and measured affection by the depth of awe it inspired.

"'My daughter!' broke from his lips, and he never inquired who she was or what; no, not even when after a moment of silence she raised her head and with a sudden low cry of passionate longing looked in his face and murmured,

"'I never had a father.'

"Sirs, it is impossible for me to continue without revealing depths of pride and bitterness in my own nature, from which I now shrink with unspeakable pain. So far from being touched by this scene, I felt myself grow hard under it. If he had been disappointed in my choice, queried at it or even been simply pleased at my obedience, I might have accepted the wife I had won, and been tolerably grateful. But to love her, admire her, glory in her when Evelyn Blake had never succeeded in winning a glance from his eyes that was not a public disapprobation! I could not endure it; my whole being rebelled, and a movement like hate took possession of me.

"Bidding my wife to leave me with my father alone, I scarcely waited for the door to close upon the poor young thing before all that had been seething in my breast for a month, burst from me in the one cry,

"'I have brought you a daughter as you commanded me. Now give me the blessing you promised and let me go; for I cannot live with a woman I do not love.'

"Instantly, and before his lips could move, the door opened and the woman I thus repudiated in the first dawning hour of her young bliss, stood before us. My

God! what a face! When I think of it now in the night season—when from dreams that gloomy as they are, are often elysian to the thoughts which beset me in my waking hours, I suddenly arouse to see starting upon me from the surrounding shadows that young fair brow with its halo of golden tresses, blotted, ay blotted by the agony that turned her that instant into stone, I wonder I did not take out the pistol that lay in the table near which I stood, and shoot her lifeless on the spot as some sort of a compensation for the misery I had caused her. I say I wonder now: then I only thought of braving it out.

"Straight as a dart, but with that look on her face, she came towards us. 'Did I hear aright?' were the words that came from her lips. 'Have you married me, a woman beneath your station as I now perceive, because you were commanded to do so? Have you not loved me? given me that which alone makes marriage a sacrament or even a possibility? and must you leave this house made sacred by the recumbent form of your dying father if I remain within it?'

"I saw my father's stiff and pallid lips move silently as though he would answer for me if he could, and summoning up what courage I possessed, I told her that I deeply regretted she had overheard my inconsiderate words. That I had never meant to wound her, whatever bitterness lay in my heart towards one who had thwarted me in my dearest and most cherished hopes. That I humbly begged her pardon and would so far acknowledge her claim upon me as to promise that I would not leave my home at this time, if it distressed her; my desire being not to injure her, only to protect myself.

"O the scorn that mounted to her brow at these weak words. Not scorn of me, thank God, worthy as I was of it that hour, but scorn of my slight opinion of her.

"'Then I heard aright,' she murmured, and waited with a look that would not be gainsaid.

"I could only bow my head, cursing the day I was born.

"'Holman! Holman!' came in agonized entreaty from the bed, 'you will not rob me of my daughter now?'

"Startled, I looked up. Luttra was half way to the door.

"'What are you going to do?' cried I, bounding towards her.

"She stopped me with a look. 'The son must never forsake the father,' said she. 'If either of us must leave the house this day, let it be I.' Then in a softer tone, 'When you asked me to be your wife, I who had worshipped you from the moment you entered my father's house on the memorable night I left it, was so overcome at your condescension that I forgot you did not preface it by the usual passionate, 'I love you,' which more than the marriage ring binds two hearts together. In the glamour and glow of my joy, I did not see that the smile that was in my heart, was missing from your face. I was to be your wife and that was enough, or so I thought then, for I loved you. Ah, and I do now, my husband, love you so that I leave you. Were it for your happiness I would do more than that, I would give you back your freedom, but from what I hear, it seems that you need a wife in name and I will be but fulfilling your desire in holding that place for you. I will never disgrace the position high as it is above my poor deserts. When the day comes—if the day comes—that you need or feel you need the sustainment of my presence or the devotion of my heart, no power on earth save that of death itself, shall keep me from your side. Till that day arrives I remain what you have made me, a bride who lays no claim to the name you this morning bestowed upon her.' And with a gesture that was like a benediction, she turned, and noiselessly, breathlessly as a dream that vanishes, left the room.

"Sirs, I believe I uttered a cry and stumbled towards her. Some one in that room uttered a cry, but it may be that it only rose in my heart and that the one I heard came from my father's lips. For when at the door I turned, startled at the deathly silence, I saw he had fainted on his pillow. I could not leave him so. Calling to Mrs. Daniels, who was never far from my father in those days, I bade her stop the lady—I believe I called her my wife—who was going down the stairs, and then rushed to his side. It took minutes to revive him. When he came to himself it was to ask for the creature who had flashed like a beacon of light upon his darkening path. I rose as if to fetch her but before I could advance I heard a voice say, 'She is not here,' and looking up I saw Mrs. Daniels glide into the room.

"'Mrs. Blake has gone, sir, I could not keep her.'"

CHAPTER XIII.

A MAN'S HEART

"That was the last time my eyes ever rested upon my wife. Whither she went or what refuge she gained, I never knew. My father who had received in this scene a great shock, began to fail so rapidly, he demanded my constant care; and though from time to time as I ministered to him and noted with what a yearning persistency he would eye the door and then turn and meet my gaze with a look I could not understand, I caught myself asking whether I had done a deed destined to hang forever about me like a pall; it was not till after his death that the despairing image of the bright young creature to whom I had given my name, returned with any startling distinctness to my mind, or that I allowed myself to ask whether the heavy gloom which I now felt settling upon me was owing to the sense of shame that overpowered me at the remembrance of the past, or to the possible loss I had sustained in the departure of my young unloved bride.

"The announcement at this time of the engagement between Evelyn Blake and the Count De Mirac may have had something to do with this. Though I had never in the most passionate hours of my love for her, lost sight of that side of her nature which demanded as her right the luxury of great wealth; and though in my tacit abandonment of her and secret marriage with another I had certainly lost the right to complain of her actions whatever they might be, this manifest surrendering of herself to the power of wealth and show at the price of all that women are believed to hold dear, was an undoubted blow to my pride and the confidence I had till now unconsciously reposed in her inherent womanliness and affection. That she had but made on a more conspicuous scale, the same sacrifice as myself to the god of Wealth and Position, was in my eyes at that time, no palliation of her conduct. I was a man none too good or exalted at the best; she, a woman, should have been superior to the temptations that overpowered me. That she was not, seemed to drag all womanhood a little nearer the dust; fashionable womanhood I ought to say, for somehow even at that early day her conduct did not seem to affect the vivid image of Luttra standing upon my threshold, shorn of her joy but burning with a devotion I did not comprehend, and saying,

"'I loved you. Ah, and I do yet, my husband, love you so that I leave you. When the day comes—if the day comes—you need or feel you need the sustainment of my presence or the devotion of my heart, no power on earth save that of death itself, shall keep me from your side.'

"Yes, with the fading away of other faces and other forms, that face and that form now began to usurp the chief place in my thoughts. Not to my relief and pleasure. That could scarcely be, remembering all that had occurred; rather to my increasing distress and passionate resentment. I longed to forget I was held by a tie, that known to the world would cause me the bitterest shame. For by this time the true character of her father and brother had been revealed and I found myself bound to the daughter of a convicted criminal.

"But I could not forget her. The look with which she had left me was branded into my consciousness. Night and day it floated before me, till to escape it I re-solved to fasten it upon canvas, if by that means I might succeed in eliminating it from my dreams.

"The painting you have seen this night is the result. Born with an artist's touch and insight that under other circumstances might, perhaps, have raised me into the cold dry atmosphere of fame, the execution of this piece of work, presented but few difficulties to my somewhat accustomed hand. Day by day her beauty grew beneath my brush, startling me often with its spiritual force and significance till my mind grew feverish over its work, and I could scarcely refrain from rising at night to give a touch here or there to the floating golden hair or the piercing, tender eyes turned, ah, ever turned upon the inmost citadel of my heart with that look that slew my father before his time and made me, yes me, old in spirit even in the ardent years of my first manhood.

"At last it was finished and she stood before me life-like and real in the very garments and with almost the very aspect of that never to be forgotten moment. Even the roses which in the secret uneasiness of my conscience I had put in her hand on our departure from Troy, as a sort of visible token that I regarded her as my bride, and which through all her interview with my father she had never dropped, blossomed before me on the canvas. Nothing that could give reality to the likeness, was lacking; the vision of my dreams stood embodied in my sight, and I looked for peace. Alas, that picture now became my dream.

"Inserting it behind that of Evelyn which for two years had held its place above my armchair, I turned its face to the wall when I rose in the morning. But at night it beamed ever upon me, becoming as the months passed, the one thing to hold to and muse over when the world grew a little noisy in my ears and the never ceasing conflict of the ages beat a trifle too loudly on heart and brain.

"Meanwhile no word of her, only of her villainous father and brother; no to-ken that she had escaped evil or was removed from want. If I had loved her I could not have succored her, for I did not know where to find her. Her countenance illumined my wall, but her fair young self lay for all I knew sheltered within the darkness and silence of the tomb.

"At length my morbid broodings worked out their natural result. A dull mel-ancholy settled upon me which nothing could break. Even the news that my cous-in who had lost her husband a month after marriage, had returned to America with expectation to remain, scarcely caused a ripple in my apathy. Was I sinking into a hypochrondriac? or was my passion for the beautiful brunette dead? I deter-mined to solve the doubt.

"Seeking her where I knew she would be found, I gazed again upon her beauty. It was absolutely nothing to me. A fair young face with high thoughts in every glance floated like sunshine between us and I left the haughty Countess, with the knowledge burned deep into my brain, that the love I had considered slain was alive and demanding, but that the object of it past recall, was my lost young wife.

"Once assured of this, my apathy vanished like mist before a kindled torch. Henceforth the future held a hope, and life a purpose. I would seek my wife throughout the world and bring her back if I found her in prison between the men whose existence was a curse to my pride. But where should I turn my steps? What golden thread had she left in my hand by which to trace her through the labyrinth of this world? I could think of but one, and that was the love which would restrain her from going away from me too far. The Luttra of old would not leave the city where her husband lived. If she was not changed, I ought to be able to find her somewhere within this great Babylon of ours. Wisdom told me to set the police upon her track, but pride bade me try every other means first. So with the feverish energy of one leading a forlorn hope, I began to pace the streets if haply I might see her face shine upon me from the crowd of passers by; a foolish fancy, unproductive of result! I not only failed to see her, but anyone like her.

"In the midst of the despair occasioned by this failure a thought flashed across me or rather a remembrance. One night not long since, being uncommonly restless, I had risen from my bed, dressed me and gone out into the yard back of my house for a little air. It was an unusual thing for me to do but I seemed to be suffocating where I was, and nothing else would satisfy me. As you already surmise, it was the night on which disappeared the sewing girl of which you have so often spoken, but I knew nothing of that, my thoughts were far from my own home and its concerns. You may judge what a state of mind I was in when I tell you that I even thought at one moment while I paused before the gate leading into — — Street that I saw the face of her with whom my thoughts were ever busy, peering upon me through the bars.

"You tell me that I did see a girl there, and that it was the one who had lived as sewing woman in my house; it may be so, but at the time I considered it a vision of my wife, and the remembrance of it, coming as it did after my repeated failures to encounter her in the street, worked a change in my plans. For regard it as weakness or not, the recollection that the vision I had seen wore the garments of a working-woman rather than a lady, acted upon me like a warning not to search for her any longer among the resorts of the well-dressed, but in the regions of poverty and toil. I therefore took to wanderings such as I have no heart to describe. Nor do I need to, if, as you have informed me, I have been followed.

"The result was almost madness. Though deep in my heart I felt a steadfast trust in the purity of her intentions, the fear of what she might have been driven to by the awful poverty and despair I every day saw seething about me, was like hot steel in brain and heart. Then her father and her brother! To what might they not have forced her, innocent and loving soul though she was! Drinking the dregs of a cup such as I had never considered it possible for me to taste, I got so far as to believe that her eyes would yet flash upon me from beneath some of the tattered shawls I saw sullying the forms of the young girls upon which I hourly stumbled. Yes, and even made a move to see my cousin, if haply I could so win upon her compassion as to gain her consent to shelter the poor creature of my dreams in case the necessity came. But my heart failed me at the sight of her cold face above the splendor she had bought with her charms, and I was saved a humiliation I might never have risen above.

"At last, one day I saw a girl—no, it was not she, but her hair was similar to hers in hue, and the impulse to follow her was irresistible. I did more than that, I spoke to her. I asked her if she could tell me anything of one whose locks were golden red like hers—But I need not tell you what I said nor what she replied with a gentle delicacy that was almost a shock to me as showing from what heights to what depths a woman can fall. Enough that nothing passed between us beyond what I have intimated, and that in all she said she gave me no news of Luttra.

"Next day I started for the rambling old house in Vermont, if haply in the spot where I first saw her, I might come upon some clue to her present whereabouts. But the old inn was deserted, and whatever hope I may have had in that direction, perished with the rest.

"Concerning the contents of that bureau-drawer above, I can say nothing. If, as I scarcely dare to hope, they should prove to have been indeed brought here by the girl who has since disappeared so strangely, who knows but what in those folded garments a clue is given which will lead me at last to the knowledge for which I would now barter all I possess. My wife—But I can mention her name no more till the question that now assails us is set at rest. Mrs. Daniels must—"

But at that moment the door opened and Mrs. Daniels came in.

CHAPTER XIV.

MRS. DANIELS

She still wore her bonnet and shawl and her face was like marble.

"You want me?" said she with a hurried look towards Mr. Blake that had as much fear as surprise in it.

"Yes," murmured that gentleman moving towards her with an effort we could very well appreciate. "Mrs. Daniels, who was the girl you harbored in that room above us for so long? Speak; what was her name and where did she come from?"

The housekeeper trembling in every limb, cast us one hurried appeal.

"Speak!" reechoed Mr. Gryce; "the time for secrecy has passed."

"O," cried she, sinking into a chair from sheer inability to stand, "it was your wife, Mr. Blake, the young creature you—"

"Ah!"

All the agony, the hopelessness, the love, the passion of those last few months flashed up in that word. She stopped as if she had been shot, but seeing the hand which he had hurriedly raised, fall slowly before him, went on with a burst,

"O sir, she made me swear on my knees I would never betray her, no matter what happened. When not two weeks after your father died she came to the house and asking for me, told me all her story and all her love; how she could not reconcile it with her idea of a wife's duty to live under any other roof than that of her husband, and lifting off the black wig which she wore, showed me how altered she had made herself by that simple change—in her case more marked by the fact that her eyes were in keeping with black hair, while with her own bright locks they always gave you a shock as of something strange and haunting—I gave up my will as if forced by a magnetic power, and not only opened the house to her but my heart as well; swearing to all she demanded and keeping my oath too, as I would preserve my soul from sin and my life from the knife of the destroyer."

"But, when she went," broke from the pallid lips of the man before her, "when she was taken away from the house, what then?"

"Ah," returned the agitated woman, "what then! Do you not think I suffered? To be held by my oath, an oath I was satisfied she would wish kept even at this crisis, yet knowing all the while she was drifting away into some evil that you, if you knew who she was, would give your life to avert from your honor if not from her innocent head! To see you cold, indifferent, absorbed in other things, while she, who would have perished any day for your happiness, was losing her life perhaps in the clutches of those horrible villains! Do not ask me to tell you what I have suffered since she went; I can never tell you,—innocent, tender, noble-hearted creature that she was."

"Was?" His hand clutched his heart as if it had been seized by a deathly spasm. "Why do you say was?"

"Because I have just come from the Morgue where she lies dead."

"No, no," came in a low shriek from his lips, "that is not she; that is another woman, like her perhaps, but not she."

"Would to God you were right; but the long golden braids! Such hair as hers I never saw on anyone before."

"Mr. Blake is right," I broke in, for I could not endure this scene any longer. "The woman taken out of the East river to-day has been both seen and spoken to by him and that not long since. He should know if it is his wife."

"And isn't it?"

"No, a thousand times no; the girl was a perfect stranger."

The assurance seemed to lift a leaden weight from her heart. "O thank God," she murmured dropping with an irresistible impulse on her knees. Then with a sudden return of her old tremble, "But I was only to reveal her secret in case of her death! What have I done, O what have I done! Her only hope lay in my faithfulness."

Mr. Blake leaning heavily on the table before him, looked in her face.

"Mrs. Daniels," said he, "I love my wife; her hope now lies in me."

She leaped to her feet with a joyous bound. "You love her? O thank God!" she again reiterated but this time in a low murmur to her self. "Thank God!" and weeping with unrestrained joy, she drew back into a corner.

Of course after that, all that remained for us to do was to lay our heads together and consult as to the best method of renewing our search after the unhappy girl, now rendered of double interest to us by the facts with which we had just been made acquainted. That she had been forced away from the roof that sheltered her by the power of her father and brother was of course no longer open to doubt. To discover them, therefore, meant to recover her. Do you wonder, then, that from the moment we left Mr. Blake's house, the capture of that brace of thieves became the leading purpose of our two lives?

CHAPTER XV.

A CONFAB

Next morning Mr. Gryce and I met in serious consultation. How, and in what direction should we extend the inquiries necessary to a discovery of these Schoen-makers?

"I advise a thorough overhauling of the German quarter," said my superior. "Schmidt, and Rosenthal will help us and the result ought to be satisfactory."

But I shook my head at this. "I don't believe," said I, "that they will hide among their own people. You must remember they are not alone, but have with them a young woman of a somewhat distinguished appearance, whose presence in a crowded district, like that, would be sure to awaken gossip; something which above all else they must want to avoid."

"That is true; the Germans are a dreadful race for gossip."

"If they dared to ill-dress her or ill-treat her, it would be different. But she is a valuable piece of property to them you see, a choice lot of goods which it is for their interest to preserve in first-class condition till the day comes for its disposal. For I presume you have no doubt that it is for the purpose of extorting money from Mr. Blake that they have carried off his young wife."

"For that reason or one similar. He is a man of resources, they may have hoped he would help them to escape the country."

"If they don't hide in the German quarter they certainly won't in the Italian, French or Irish. What they want is too keep close and rouse no questions. I think they will be found to have gone up the river somewhere, or over to Jersey. Hoboken would'nt be a bad place to send Schmidt to."

"You forget what it is they've got on their minds; besides no conspicuous party such as they could live in a rural district without attracting more attention than in the most crowded tenement house in the city."

"Where do you think, then, they would be liable to go?"

"Well my most matured thought on the subject," returned Mr. Gryce, after a moment's deliberation, "is this,—you say, and I agree, that they have hampered themselves with this woman at this time for the purpose of using her hereafter in a scheme of black-mail upon Mr. Blake. He, then, must be the object about which their thoughts revolve and toward which whatever operations or plans they may be engaged upon must tend. What follows? When a company of men have made up their minds to rob a bank, what is the first thing they do? They hire, if possible, a house next to the especial building they intend to enter, and for months work upon the secret passage through which they hope to reach the safe and its contents; or they make friends with the watchman that guards its treasures, and the janitor who opens and shuts the doors. In short they hang about their prey before they pounce upon it. And so will these Schoenmakers do in the somewhat different robbery which they plan sooner or later to effect. Whatever may keep them close at this moment, Mr. Blake and Mr. Blake's house is the point toward which their eyes are turned, and if we had time—"

"But we have'nt," I broke in impetuously. "It is horrible to think of that grand woman languishing away in the power of such rascals."

"If we had time," Mr. Gryce persisted, "all it would be necessary to do would be to wait, they would come into our hands as easily and naturally as a hawk into the snare of the fowler. But as you say we have not, and therefore, I would recommend a little beating of the bush directly about Mr. Blake's house; for if all my experience is not at fault, those men are already within eye-shot of the prey they intend to run down."

"But," said I, "I have been living myself in that very neighborhood and know by this time the ways of every house in the vicinity. There is not a spot up and down the Avenue for ten blocks where they could hide away for two days much less two weeks. And as for the side streets,—why I could tell you the names of those who live in each house for a considerable distance. Yet if you say so I will go to work—"

"Do, and meanwhile Schmidt and Rosenthal shall rummage the German quarter and even go through Williamsburgh and Hoboken. The end justifies any amount of labor that can be spent upon this matter."

"And you," I asked.

"Will do my part when you have done yours."

CHAPTER XVI.

THE MARK OF THE RED CROSS

And what success did I meet? The best in the world. And by what means did I attain it? By that of the simplest, prettiest clue I ever came upon. But let me explain.

When after a wearisome day spent in an ineffectual search through the neighborhood, I went home to my room, which as you remember was a front one in a lodging-house on the opposite corner from Mr. Blake, I was so absorbed in mind and perhaps I may say shaken in nerve, by the strain under which I had been laboring for some time now, that I stumbled up an extra flight of stairs, and without any suspicion of the fact, tried the door of the room directly over mine. It is a wonder to me now that I could have made the mistake, for the halls were totally dissimilar, the one above being much more cut up than the one below, besides being flanked by a greater number of doors. But the intoxication of the mind is not far removed from that of the body, and as I say it was not till I had tried the door and found it locked, that I became aware of the mistake I had made.

With the foolish sense of shame that always overcomes us at the committal of any such trivial error, I stumbled hastily back, when my foot trod upon something that broke under my weight. I never let even small things pass without some notice. Stooping, then, for what I had thus inadvertently crushed, I carried it to where a single gas jet turned down very low, made a partial light in the long hall, and examining it, found it to be a piece of red chalk.

What was there in that simple fact to make me start and hastily recall one or two half-forgotten incidents which, once brought to mind, awoke a train of thought that led to the discovery and capture of those two desperate thieves? I will tell you.

I don't remember now whether in my account of the visit I paid to the Schoenmakers' house in Vermont, I informed you of the red cross I noticed scrawled on the panel of one of the doors. It seemed a trivial thing at the time and made little or no impression upon me, the chances being that I should never have thought of it again, if I had not come upon the article just mentioned at a moment when my mind was full of those very Schoenmakers. But remembered now, together with another half-forgotten fact, — that some days previous I had been told by the woman who kept the house I was in, that the parties over my head (two men and a woman I believe she said) were giving her some trouble, but that they paid well and therefore she did not like to turn them out, — it aroused a vague suspicion in my mind, and led to my walking back to the door I had endeavored to open in my abstraction, and carefully looking at it.

It was plain and white, rather ruder of make than those below, but offering no inducements for prolonged scrutiny. But not so with the one that stood at right angles to it on the left. Full in the centre of that, I beheld distinctly scrawled, probably with the very piece of chalk I then held, a red cross precisely similar in outline to the one I had seen a few days before on the panel of the Schoenmakers' door at Granby.

The discovery sent a thrill over me that almost raised my hair on end. Was, then, this famous trio to be found in the very house in which I had been myself living for a week or more? over my head in fact? I could not withdraw my gaze from the mysterious looking object. I bent near, I listened, I heard what sounded like the suppressed snore of a powerful man, and almost had to lay hold of myself to prevent my hand from pushing open that closed door and my feet from entering. As it was I did finger the knob a little, but an extra loud snore from within reminded me by its suggestion of strength that I was but a small man and that in this case and at this hour, discretion was the better part of valor.

I therefore withdrew, but for the whole night lay awake listening to catch any sounds that might come from above, and going so far as to plan what I would do if it should be proved that I was indeed upon the trail of the men I was so anxious to encounter.

With the breaking of day I was upon my feet. A rude step had gone up the stairs a few minutes before and I was all alert to follow. But I presently considered that my wisest course would be to sound the landlady and learn if possible with what sort of characters I had to deal. Routing her out of the kitchen, where at that early hour she was already engaged in domestic duties, I drew her into a retired corner and put my questions. She was not backward in replying. She had conceived an innocent liking for me in the short time I had been with her — a display of weakness for which I was myself, perhaps, as much to blame as she — and was only too ready to pour out her griefs into my sympathizing ear. For those men were a grief to her, acceptable as was the money they were careful to provide her with. They were not only always in the house, that is one of them, smoking his old pipe and blackening up the walls, but they looked so shabby, and kept the girl so close, and if they did go out, came in at such unheard of hours. It was enough to drive her crazy; yet the money, the money —

"Yes," said I, "I know; and the money ought to make you overlook all the small disagreeablenesses you mention. What is a landlady without patience." And I urged her not to turn them out.

"But the girl," she went on, "so nice, so quiet, so sick-looking! I cannot stand it to see her cooped up in that small room, always watched over by one or both of those burly wretches. The old man says she is his daughter and she does not deny it, but I would as soon think of that little rosy child you see cooing in the window over the way, belonging to the beggar going in at the gate, as of her with her lady-like ways having any connection with him and his rough-acting son. You ought to see her —"

"That is just what I want to do," interrupted I. "Not because you have tempted my fancy by a recital of her charms," I hastened to add, "but because she is, if I don't mistake, a woman for whose discovery and rescue, a large sum of money has been offered."

And without further disguise I acquainted the startled woman before me with the fact that I was not, as she had always considered, the clerk out of employment whose daily business it was to sally forth in quest of a situation, but a member of the city police.

She was duly impressed and easily persuaded to second all my operations as far as her poor wits would allow, giving me free range of her upper story, and above all, promising that secrecy without which all my finely laid plans for capturing the rogues without raising a scandal, would fall headlong to the ground.

Behold me, then, by noon of that same day domiciled in an apartment next to the one whose door bore that scarlet sign which had aroused within me such feverish hopes the night before. Clad in the seedy garments of a broken down French artist whose acquaintance I had once made, with something of his air and general appearance and with a few of his wretched daubs hung about on the whitewashed wall, I commenced with every prospect of success as I thought, that quiet espionage of the hall and its inhabitants which I considered necessary to a proper attainment of the end I had in view.

A racking cough was one of the peculiarities of my friend, and determined to assume the character in toto, I allowed myself to startle the silence now and then with a series of gasps and chokings that whether agreeable or not, certainly were of a character to show that I had no desire to conceal my presence from those I had come among. Indeed it was my desire to acquaint them as fully and as soon as possible with the fact of their having a neighbor: a weak-eyed half-alive innocent to be sure, but yet a neighbor who would keep his door open night and day—for the warmth of the hall of course—and who with the fretful habit of an old man who had once been a gentleman and a beau, went rambling about through the hall speaking to those he met and expecting a civil word in return. When he was not rambling or coughing he made architectural monsters out of cardboard, wherewith to tempt the pennies out of the pockets of unwary children, an employment that kept him chained to a small table in the centre of his room directly opposite the open door.

As I expected I had scarcely given way to three separate fits of coughing, when the door next me opened with a jerk and a rough voice called out,

"Who's that making all that to do about here? If you don't stop that infernal noise in a hurry—"

A soft voice interrupted him and he drew back. "I will go see," said those gentle tones, and Luttra Blake, for I knew it was she before the skirt of her robe had advanced beyond the door, stepped out into the hall.

I was yet bent over my work when she paused before me. The fact is I did not dare look up, the moment was one of such importance to me.

"You have a dreadful cough," said she with that low ring of sympathy in her voice that goes unconsciously to the heart. "Is there no help for it?"

I pushed back my work, drew my hand over my eyes, (I did not need to make it tremble) and glanced up. "No," said I with a shake of my head, "but it is not always so bad. I beg your pardon, miss, if it disturbs you."

She threw back the shawl which she had held drawn tightly over her head, and advanced with an easy gliding step close to my side. "You do not disturb me, but my father is—is, well a trifle cross sometimes, and if he should speak up a little harsh now and then, you must not mind. I am sorry you are so ill."

What is there in some women's look, some women's touch that more than all beauty goes to the heart and subdues it. As she stood there before me in her dark worsted dress and coarse shawl, with her locks simply braided and her whole person undignified by art and ungraced by ornament, she seemed just by the power of her expression and the witchery of her manner, the loveliest woman I had ever beheld.

"You are veree kind, veree good," I murmured, half ashamed of my disguise, though it was assumed for the purpose of rescuing her. "Your sympathy goes to my heart." Then as a deep growl of impatience rose from the room at my side, I motioned her to go and not irritate the man who seemed to have such control over her.

"In a minute," answered she, "first tell me what you are making."

So I told her and in the course of telling, let drop such other facts about my fancied life as I wished to have known to her and through her to her father. She looked sweetly interested and more than once turned upon me that dark eye, of which I had heard so much, full of tears that were as much for me, scamp that I was, as for her own secret trouble. But the growls becoming more and more impatient she speedily turned to go, repeating, however, as she did so,

"Now remember what I say, you are not to be troubled if they do speak cross to you. They make noise enough themselves sometimes, as you will doubtless be assured of to-night."

And the lips which seemed to have grown stiff and cold with her misery, actually softened into something like a smile.

The nod which I gave her in return had the solemnity of a vow in it.

My mind thus assured as to the correctness of my suspicions, and the way thus paved to the carrying out of my plans, I allowed some few days to elapse without further action on my part. My motive was to acquaint myself as fully as possible with the habits and ways of these two desperate men, before making the attempt to capture them upon which so many interests hung. For while I felt it would be highly creditable to my sagacity, as well as valuable to my reputation as a detective, to restore these escaped convicts in any way possible into the hands of justice, my chief ambition after all was to so manage the affair as to save the wife of Mr. Blake, not only from the consequences of their despair, but from the publicity and scandal attendant upon the open arrest of two heavily armed men. Strategy, therefore, rather than force was to be employed, and strategy to be successful must be founded upon the most thorough knowledge of the matter with which one has to deal. Three days, then, did I give to the acquiring of that knowledge, the result of which was the possession of the following facts.

1. That the landlady was right when she told me the girl was never left alone, one of the men, if not the father then the son, always remaining with her.

2. That while thus guarded, she was not so restricted but that she had the liberty of walking in the hall, though never for any length of time.

3. That the cross on the door seemed to possess some secret meaning connected with their presence in the house, it having been erased one evening when the whole three went out on some matter or other, only to be chalked on again when in an hour or so later, father and daughter returned alone.

4. That it was the father and not the son who made such purchases as were needed, while it was the son and not the father who carried on whatever operations they had on hand; nightfall being the favorite hour for the one and midnight for the other; though it not infrequently happened that the latter sauntered out for a short time also in the afternoon, probably for the drink he could not go long without.

5. That they were men of great strength but little alertness; the stray glimpses I had had of them, revealing a breadth of back that was truly formidable, if it had not been joined to a heaviness of motion that proclaimed a certain stolidity of mind that was eminently in our favor.

How best to use these facts in the building up of a matured plan of action, was, then, the problem. By noon of a certain day I believed it to have been solved, and reluctant as I was to leave the spot of my espionage even for the hour or two necessary to a visit to headquarters, I found myself compelled to do so. Packing up in a small basket I had for the purpose, the little articles I had been engaged during the last few days in making, I gave way to a final fit of coughing so hollow and sepulchral in its tone, that it awoke a curse from the next room deep as the growl of a wild beast, and still continuing, finally brought Luttra to the door with that look of compassion on her face that always called up a flush to my cheek whether I wished it or no.

"Ah, Monsieur, I am afraid your cough is very bad to-day. O I see; you have been getting ready to go out—"

"Come back here," broke in a heavy voice from the room she had left. "What do you mean by running off to palaver with that old rascal every time he opens his ——- battery of a cough?"

A smile that went through me like the cut of a knife, flashed for a moment on her face.

"My father is in one of his impatient moods," said she, "you had better go. I hope you will be successful," she murmured, glancing wistfully at my basket.

"What is that?" again came thundering on our ears. "Successful? What are you two up to?" And we heard the rough clatter of advancing steps.

"Go," said she; "you are weak and old; and when you come back, try and not cough." And she gave me a gentle push towards the door.

"When I come back," I began, but was forced to pause, the elder Schoenmaker having by this time reached the open doorway where he stood frowning in upon us in a way that made my heart stand still for her.

"What are you two talking about?" said he; "and what have you got in your basket there?" he continued with a stride forward that shook the floor.

"Only some little toys that he has been making, and is now going out to sell," was her low answer given with a quick deprecatory gesture such as I doubt if she ever used for herself.

"Nothing more?" asked he in German with a red glare in the eye he turned towards her.

"Nothing more," replied she in the same tongue. "You may believe me."

He gave a deep growl and turned away. "If there was," said he, "you know what would happen." And unheeding the wild keen shudder that seized her at the word, making her insensible for the moment to all and everything about her, he laid one heavy hand upon her slight shoulder and led her from the room.

I waited no longer than was necessary to carry my feeble and faltering steps appropriately down the stairs, to reach the floor below and gain the landlady's presence.

"Do you go up," said I, "and sit on those stairs till I come back. If you hear the least cry of pain or sound of struggle from that young girl's room, do you call at once for help. I will have a policeman standing on the corner below."

The good woman nodded and proceeded at once to take up her work-basket. "Lucky there's a window up there, so I can see," I heard her mutter. "I've no time to throw away even on deeds of charity."

Notwithstanding which precaution, I was in constant anxiety during my absence; an absence necessarily prolonged as I had to stop and explain matters to the Superintendent, as well as hunt up Mr. Gryce and get his consent to assist me in the matter of the impending arrest.

I found the latter in his own home and more than enthusiastic upon the subject.

"Well," said he after I had informed him of the discoveries I had made, "the fates seem to prosper you in this. I have not received an inkling of light upon the matter since I parted from you at Mr. Blake's house. By the way I saw that gentleman this morning and I tell you we will find him a grateful man if this affair can be resolved satisfactorily."

"That is good," said I," gratitude is what we want." Then shortly, "Perhaps it is no more than our duty to let him know that his wife is safe and under my eye; though I would by no means advocate his knowing just how near him she is, till the moment comes when he is wanted, or we shall have a lover's impetuosity to deal with as well as all the rest." Then with a hurried remembrance of a possible contingency, went on to say, "But, by the way, in case we should need the cooperation of Mrs. Blake in what we have before us, you had better get a line written in French from Mrs. Daniels, expressive of her belief in Mr. Blake's present affection for his wife. The latter will not otherwise trust us, or understand that we are to be obeyed in whatever we may demand. Let it be unsigned and without names in case of accident; and if the housekeeper don't understand French, tell her to get some one to help her that does, only be sure that the handwriting employed is her own."

Mr. Gryce seemed to perceive the wisdom of this precaution and promised to procure me such a note by a certain hour, after which I related to him the various other details of the capture such as I had planned it, meeting to my secret gratification an unqualified approval that went far towards alleviating that wound to my pride which I had received from him in the beginning of this affair.

"Let all things proceed as you have determined, and we shall accomplish something that it will be a life-long satisfaction to remember," said he; "but you must be prepared for some twist of the screw which you do not anticipate. I never knew anything to go off just as one prognosticates it must, except once," he added thoughtfully, "and then it was with a surprise attached to it that well nigh upset me notwithstanding all my preparations."

"You won a great success that day," remarked I. "I hope the fates will be as propitious to me to-morrow. Failure now would break my heart."

"But you won't fail," exclaimed he. "I myself am resolved to see you through this matter with credit."

And in this assurance I returned to my lodgings where I found the landlady sitting where I had left her, darning her twenty-third sock.

"I have to mend for a dozen men and three boys," said she, "and the boys are the worst by a heap sight. Look at that, will you," holding up a darn with a bit of stocking attached. "That hole was made playing shinny."

I uttered my condolences and asked if any sound or disturbance had reached her ears from above.

"O no, all is right up there; I've scarcely heard a whisper since you've been gone."

I gave her a pat on the chin scarcely consistent with my aged and tottering mien and proceeded to shamble painfully to my room.

CHAPTER XVII.

THE CAPTURE

Promptly next morning at the designated hour, came the little note promised me by Mr. Gryce. It was put in my hand with many sly winks by the landlady herself, who developed at this crisis quite an adaptation for, if not absolute love of intrigue and mystery. Glancing over it—it was unsealed—and finding it entirely unintelligible, I took it for granted it was all right and put it by till chance, or if that failed, strategy, should give me an opportunity to communicate with Mrs. Blake. An hour passed; the doors of their rooms remained unclosed. A half hour more dragged its slow minutes away, and no sound had come from their precincts save now and then a mumbled word of parley between the father and son, a short command to the daughter, or a not-to-be-restrained oath of annoyance from one or both of the heavy-limbed brutes as something was said or done to disturb them in their indolent repose. At last my impatience was to be no longer restrained. Rising, I took a bold resolution. If the mountain would not come to Mahomet, Mahomet would go to the mountain. Taking my letter in the hand, I deliberately proceeded to the door marked with the ominous red cross and knocked.

A surprised snarl from within, followed by a sudden shuffling of feet as the two men leaped upright from what I presume had been a recumbent position, warned me to be ready to face defiance if not the fury of despair; and curbing with a determined effort the slight sinking of heart natural to a man of my make on the threshold of a very doubtful adventure, I awaited with as much apparent unconcern as possible, the quick advance of that light foot which seemed to be ready to perform all the biddings of these hardened wretches, much as it shrunk from following in the ways of their infamy.

"Ah miss," said I, as the door opened revealing in the gap her white face clouded with some new and sudden apprehension, "I beg your pardon but I am an old man, and I got a letter to-day and my eyes are so weak with the work I've been doing that I cannot read it. It is from some one I love, and would you be so kind as to read off the words for me and so relieve an old man from his anxiety."

The murmur of suspicion behind her, warned her to throw wide open the door. "Certainly," said she, "if I can," taking the paper in her hand.

"Just let me get a squint at that first," said a sullen voice behind her; and the youngest of the two Schoenmakers stepped forward and tore the paper out of her grasp.

"You are too suspicious," murmured she, looking after him with the first assumption of that air of power and determination which I had heard so eloquently described by the man who loved her. "There is nothing in those lines which concerns us; let me have them back."

"You hold your tongue," was the brutal reply as the rough man opened the folded paper and read or tried to read what was written within. "Blast it! it's French," was his slow exclamation after a moment spent in this way. "See," and he thrust it towards his father who stood frowning heavily a few feet off.

"Of course, it's French," cried the girl. "Would you write a note in English to father there? The man's friends are French like himself, and must write in their own language."

"Here take it and read it out," commanded her father; "and mind you tell us what it means. I'll have nothing going on here that I don't understand."

"Read me the French words first, miss," said I. "It is my letter and I want to know what my friend has to say to me."

Nodding at me with a gentle look, she cast her eyes on the paper and began to read:

"Calmez vous, mon amie, il vous aime et il vous cherche. Dans quatre heures vous serez heureuse. Allons du courage, et surtout soyez maitre de vous meme."

"Thanks!" I exclaimed in a calm matter-of-fact way as I perceived the sudden tremor that seized her as she recognized the handwriting and realized that the words were for her. "My friend says he will pay my week's rent and bids me be at home to receive him," said I, turning upon the two ferocious faces peering over her shoulder, with a look of meek unsuspiciousness in my eye, that in a theatre would have brought down the house.

"Is that what those words say, you?" asked the father, pointing over her shoulder to the paper she held.

"I will translate for you word by word what it says," replied she, nerving herself for the crisis till her face was like marble, though I could see she could not prevent the gleam of secret rapture that had visited her, from flashing fitfully across it. "Calmez vous, mon amie. Do not be afraid, my friend. Il vous aime et il vous cherche. He loves you and is hunting for you. Dans quatre heures vous serez heureuse. In four hours you will be happy. Allons du courage, et surtout soyez maitre de vous meme. Then take courage and above all preserve your self-possession. It is the French way of expressing one's self," observed she. "I am glad your friend is disposed to help you," she continued, giving me back the letter with a smile. "I am afraid you needed it."

In a sort of maze I folded up the letter, bowed my very humble thanks to her and shuffled slowly back. The fact is I had no words; I was utterly dumbfounded. Half way through that letter, with whose contents you must remember I was unacquainted, I would have given my whole chance of expected reward to have stopped her. Read out such words as those before these men! Was she crazy? But how naturally at the conclusion did she with a word make its language seem consistent with the meaning I had given it. With a fresh sense of my obligation to her,

I hurried to my room, there to count out the minutes of another long hour in anxious expectation of her making that endeavor to communicate with me, which her new hopes and fears must force her to feel almost necessary to her existence. At length, my confidence in her was rewarded. Coming out into the hall, she hurried past my door, her finger on her lip. I immediately rose and stood on the threshold with another paper in my hand, which I had prepared against this opportunity. As she glided back, I put it in her hand, and warning her with a look not to speak, resumed my usual occupation. The words I had written were as follows:

At or as near the time as possible of your brother's going out, you are to come to this room wrapped in an extra skirt and with your shawl over your head. Leave the skirt and shawl behind you, and withdraw at once to the room at the head of the stairs. You are not to speak, and you are not to vary from the plan thus laid down. Your brother and father are to be arrested, whether or no; but if you will do as this commands, they will be arrested without bloodshed and without shame to one you know.

Her face while she read these lines, was a study, but I dared not soften toward it. Dropping the paper from her hand, she gave me one inquiring look. But I pointed determinedly to the words lying upward on the floor, and would listen to no appeal. My resolve had its effect. Bowing her head with a sorrowful gesture, she laid her hand on her heart, looked up and glided from the room. I took up that paper and tore it into bits.

And now for the first time since I had been in the house, I closed the door of my room. I had a part to perform that rendered the dropping of my disguise indispensable. The old French artist had finished his work, and henceforth must merge into Q. the detective. Shortly before two o'clock my assistants began to arrive. First, Mr. Gryce appeared on the scene and was stowed away in a large room on the other side of mine. Next, two of the most agile, as well as muscular men in the force who, thanks to having taken off their shoes in the lower hall, gained the same refuge without awakening the suspicions of those we were anxious to surprise. Lastly, the landlady who went into the closet to which I had bidden Mrs. Blake retire after leaving in my room the articles I had mentioned.

All was now ready and waiting for the departure of the youngest Schoenmaker. Would he disappoint us and remain at home that day? Had any suspicions been awakened in the stolid breasts of these men, that would serve to make them more watchful than usual against running unnecessary risks? No; at or near the time for the clock to strike two, their door opened and the tread of a lumbering foot was heard in the hall. On it came, passing my room with a rude stamping that gradually grew less distinct as the hardy rough went down the corridor, brushing the wall behind which Mr. Gryce and his men lay concealed with his thick cane, and even stopping to light his pipe in front of the small apartment where cowered our good landlady with her eternal basket of mending in her lap.

At length all was quiet, and throwing open my door, I withdrew into a small closet connected with my room, to wait with indescribable impatience, the appearance of Mrs. Blake. She came in a very few minutes, remained for an instant, and departed, leaving behind her as I had requested, the skirt and shawl in which she had left her father's presence. I at once endued myself in these articles of apparel—taking care to draw the shawl well over my head—and with a pocket handkerchief to my face, (a proceeding made natural enough by the sneeze which at that very moment I took care should assail me) walked boldly back to the room from which she had just come.

The door was of course ajar, and as I swung it open with as near a simulation of her manner as possible, the vision of her powerful father lolling on a bench directly before me, offered anything but an encouraging spectacle to my eyes. But doubling myself almost together with as ladylike an atch-ee as my masculine nostrils would allow, I succeeded in closing the door and reaching a low stool by the window without calling from him anything worse than a fretful "I hope you are not going to bark too."

I did not reply to this of course, but sat with my face turned towards the street in an attitude which I hoped would awaken his attention sufficiently to cause him to get up and come over to my side. For as he sat face to the door it would be impossible to take him by surprise, and that, now that I saw what a huge and muscular creature he was, seemed to me to be the only safe method before us. But, whether from the sullenness of his disposition or the very evident laziness of the moment, he manifested no disposition to move, and hearing or thinking I did, the stealthy advance of Mr. Gryce and his companions down the hall, I allowed myself to give way to a suppressed exclamation, and leaning forward, pressed my forehead against the pane of glass before me as if something of absorbing interest had just taken place in the street beneath.

His fears at once took alarm. Bounding up with a curse, he strode towards me, muttering,

"What's up now? What's that you are looking at?" reaching my side just as Mr. Gryce and his two men softly opened the door and with a quick leap threw their arms about him, closing upon him with a force he could not resist, desperate as he was and mighty in the huge strength of an unusually developed muscular organization.

"You, you girl there, are to blame for this!" came mingled with curses from his lips, as with one huge pant he submitted to his captors. "Only let me get my hand well upon you once—Damn it!" he suddenly exclaimed, dragging the whole three men forward in his effort to get his mouth down to my ear, "go and rub that sign out on the door or I'll—you know what I'll do well enough. Do you hear?"

Rising, still with face averted, I proceeded to do what he asked. But in another moment seeing that he had been effectually bound and gagged, I took out the piece of red chalk I had kept in my pocket, and deliberately chalked it on again, after which operation I came back and took my seat as before on the low stool by the window.

The object now was to secure the second rascal in the same way we had the first; and for this purpose Mr. Gryce ordered the now helpless giant to be dragged into the adjoining small room formerly occupied by Mrs. Blake, where he and his men likewise took up their station leaving me to confront as best I might, the surprise and consternation of the one whose return we now awaited.

I did not shrink. With that brave woman's garments drawn about me, something of her dauntless spirit seemed to invade my soul, and though I expected—But let that come in its place, I am not here to interest you in myself or my selfish thoughts.

A half hour passed; he had never lingered away so long before, or so it seemed, and I was beginning to wonder if we should have to keep up this strain of nerve for hours, when the heavy tread was again heard in the hall, and with a blow of the fist that argued anger or a brutal impatience, he flung open the door and came in, I did not turn my head.

"Where's father?" he growled, stopping where he was a foot or so from the door.

I shook my head with a slight gesture and remained looking out.

He brought his cane down on the floor with a thump. "What do you mean by sitting there staring out of the window like mad and not answering when I ask you a decent question?"

Still I made no reply.

Provoked beyond endurance, yet held in check by that vague sense of danger in the air,—which while not amounting to apprehension is often sufficient to hold back from advance the most daring foot,—he stood glaring at me in what I felt to be a very ferocious attitude, but made no offer to move. Instantly I rose and still looking out of the window, made with my hand what appeared to be a signal to some one on the opposite side of the way. The ruse was effective. With an oath that rings in my ears yet, he lifted his heavy cane and advanced upon me with a bound, only to meet the same fate as his father at the hands of the watchful detectives. Not, however, before that heavy cane came down upon my head in a way to lay me in a heap at his feet and to sow the seeds of that blinding head-ache, which has afflicted me by spells ever since. But this termination of the affair was no more than I had feared from the beginning; and indeed it was as much to protect Mrs. Blake from the wrath of these men, as from any requirements of the situation I had assumed the disguise I then wore. I therefore did not allow this mishap to greatly trouble me, unpleasant as it was at the time, but, as soon as ever I could do so, rose from the floor and throwing off my strange habiliments, proceeded to finish up to my satisfaction, the work already so successfully begun.

CHAPTER XVIII.

LOVE AND DUTY

Dismissing the men who had assisted us in the capture of these two hardy villains, we ranged our prisoners before us.

"Now," said Mr. Gryce, "no fuss and no swearing; you are in for it, and you might as well take it quietly as any other way."

"Give me a clutch on that girl, that's all," said her father, "Where is she? Let me see her; every father has a right to see his own daughter,"

"You shall see her," returned my superior, "but not till her husband is here to protect her."

"Her husband? ah, you know about that do you?" growled the heavy voice of the son. "A rich man they say he is and a proud one. Let him come and look at us lying here like dogs and say how he will enjoy having his wife's father and brother grinding away their lives in prison."

"Mr. Blake is coming," quoth Mr. Gryce, who by some preconcerted signal from the window had drawn that gentleman across the street. "He will tell you himself that he considers prison the best place for you. Blast you! but he—"

"But he, what?" inquired I, as the door opened and Mr. Blake with a pale face and agitated mien entered the room.

The wretch did not answer. Rousing from the cowering position in which they had both lain since their capture, the father and son struggled up in some sort of measure to their feet, and with hot, anxious eyes surveyed the countenance of the gentleman before them, as if they felt their fate hung upon the expression of his pallid face. The son was the first to speak.

"How do you do, brother-in-law," were his sullen and insulting words.

Mr. Blake shuddered and cast a look around.

"My wife?" murmured he.

"She is well," was the assurance given by Mr. Gryce, "and in a room not far from this. I will send for her if you say so."

"No, not yet," came in a sort of gasp; "let me look at these wretches first, and understand if I can what my wife has to suffer from her connection with them."

"Your wife," broke in the father, "what's that to do with it; the question is how do you like it and what will you do to get us clear of this thing."

"I will do nothing," returned Mr. Blake. "You amply merit your doom and you shall suffer it to the end for all time."

"It will read well in the papers," exclaimed the son.

"The papers are to know nothing about it," I broke in. "All knowledge of your connection with Mr. or Mrs. Blake is to be buried in this spot before we or you leave it. Not a word of her or him is to cross the lips of either of you from this hour. I have set that down as a condition and it has got to be kept."

"You have, have you," thundered in chorus from father and son. "And who are you to make conditions, and what do you think we are that you expect us to keep them? Can you do anymore than put us back from where we came from?"

For reply I took from my pocket the ring I had fished out of the ashes of their kitchen stove on that memorable visit to their house, and holding it up before their faces, looked them steadily in the eye.

A sudden wild glare followed by a bluish palor that robbed their countenances of their usual semblance of daring ferocity, answered me beyond my fondest hopes.

"I got that out of the stove where you had burned your prison clothing," said I. "It is a cheap affair, but it will send you to the gallows if I choose to use it against you. The pedlar—"

"Hush," exclaimed the father in a low choked tone greatly in contrast to any he had yet used in all our dealings with him. "Throw that ring out of the window and I promise to hold my tongue about any matter you don't want spoke of. I'm not a fool—"

"Nor I," was my quick reply, as I restored the ring to my pocket. "While that remains in my possession together with certain facts concerning your habits in that old house of yours which have lately been made known to me, your life hangs by a thread I can any minute snip in two. Mr. Blake here, has spent some portion of a night in your house and knows how near it lies to a certain precipice, at foot of which—"

"Mein Gott, father, why don't you say something!" leaped in cowed accents from the son's white lips. "If they want us to keep quiet, let them say so and not go talking about things that—"

"Now look here," interposed Mr. Gryce stepping before them with a look that closed their mouths at once. "I will just tell you what we propose to do. You are to go back to prison and serve your time out, there is no help for that, but as long as you behave yourselves and continue absolutely silent regarding your relationship to the wife of this gentleman, you shall have paid into a certain bank that he will name, a monthly sum that upon your dismissal from jail shall be paid you with whatever interest it may have accumulated. You are ready to promise that, are you not?" he inquired turning to Mr. Blake.

That gentleman bowed and named the sum, which was liberal enough, and the bank.

"But," continued the detective, ignoring the sudden flash of eye that passed between the father and son, "let me or any of us hear of a word having been uttered by you, which in the remotest way shall suggest that you have in the world such a connection as Mrs. Blake, and the money not only stops going into the bank, but old scores shall be raked up against you with a zeal which if it does not stop your mouth in one way, will in another, and that with a suddenness you will not altogether relish."

The men with a dogged air from which the bravado had however fled, turned and looked from one to the other of us in a fearful, inquiring way that duly confessed to the force of the impression made by these words upon their slow but not unimaginative minds.

"Do you three promise to keep our secret if we keep yours?" muttered the father with an uneasy glance at my pocket.

"We certainly do," was our solemn return.

"Very well; call in the girl and let me just look at her, then, before we go. We won't say nothing," continued he, seeing Mr. Blake shrink, "only she is my daughter and if I cannot bid her good-bye—"

"Let him see his child," cried Mr. Blake turning with a shudder to the window. "I—I wish it," added he.

Straightway with hasty foot I left the room. Going to the little closet where I had ordered his wife to remain concealed, I knocked and entered. She was crouched in an attitude of prayer on the floor, her face buried in her hands, and her whole person breathing that agony of suspense that is a torture to the sensitive soul.

"Mrs. Blake," said I, dismissing the landlady who stood in helpless distress beside her, "the arrest has been satisfactorily made and your father calls for you to say good-bye before going away with us. Will you come?"

"But my—my—Mr. Blake?" exclaimed she leaping to her feet. "I am sure I heard his footstep in the hall?"

"He is with your father and brother. It was at his command I came for you."

A gleam hard to interpret flashed for an instant over her face. With her eye on the door she towered in her womanly dignity, while thoughts innumerable seemed to rush in wild succession through her mind.

"Will you not come?" I urged.

"I—," she paused. "I will go see my father," she murmured, "but—"

Suddenly she trembled and drew back; a step was in the hall, on the threshold, at her side; Mr. Blake had come to reclaim his bride.

"Mr. Blake!"

The word came from her in a low tone shaken with the concentrated anguish of many a month of longing and despair, but there was no invitation in its sound, and he who had held out his arms, stopped and surveying her with a certain deprecatory glance in his proud eye, said,

"You are right; I have first my acknowledgments to make and your forgiveness to ask before I can hope—"

"No, no," she broke in, "your coming here is enough, I request no more. If you felt unkindly toward me—"

"Unkindly?" A world of love thrilled in that word. "Luttra, I am your husband and rejoice that I am so; it is to lay the devotion of my heart and life at your feet that I seek your presence this hour. The year has taught me—ah, what has not the year taught me of the worth of her I so recklessly threw from me on my wedding day. Luttra,"—he held out his hand—"will you crown all your other acts of devotion with a pardon that will restore me to my manhood and that place in your esteem which I covet above every other earthly good?"

Her face which had been raised to his with that earnest look we knew so well, softened with an ineffable smile, but still she did not lay her hand in his.

"And you say this to me in the very hour of my father's and brother's arrest! With the remembrance in your mind of their bound and abject forms lying before you guarded by police; knowing too, that they deserve their ignominy and the long imprisonment that awaits them?"

"No, I say it on the day of the discovery and the restoration of that wife for whom I have long searched, and to whom when found I have no word to give but welcome, welcome, welcome."

With the same deep smile she bowed her head, "Now let come what will, I can never again be unhappy," were the words I caught, uttered in the lowest of undertones. But in another moment her head had regained its steady poise and a great change had passed over her manner.

"Mr. Blake," said she, "you are good; how good, I alone can know and duly appreciate who have lived in your house this last year and seen with eyes that missed nothing, just what your surroundings are and have been from the earliest years of your proud life. But goodness must not lead you into the committal of an act you must and will repent to your dying day; or if it does, I who have learned my duty in the school of adversity, must show the courage of two and forbid what every secret instinct of my soul declares to be only provocative of shame and sorrow. You would take me to your heart as your wife; do you realize what that means?"

"I think I do," was his earnest reply. "Relief from heart-ache, Luttra."

Her smooth brow wrinkled with a sudden spasm of pain but her firm lips did not quiver.

"It means," said she, drawing nearer but not with that approach which indicates yielding, "it means, shame to the proudest family that lives in the land. It means silence as regards a past blotted by suggestions of crime; and apprehension concerning a future across which the shadow of prison walls must for so many years lie. It means, the hushing of certain words upon beloved lips; the turning of cherished eyes from visions where fathers and daughters ay, brothers and sisters are seen joined together in tender companionship or loving embrace. It means,—

God help me to speak out—a home without the sanctity of memories; a husband without the honors he has been accustomed to enjoy; a wife with a fear gnawing like a serpent into her breast; and children, yes, perhaps children from whose innocent lips the sacred word of grandfather can never fall without wakening a blush on the cheeks of their parents, which all their lovesome prattle will be helpless to chase away."

"Luttra, your father and your brother have given their consent to go their dark way alone and trouble you no more. The shadow you speak of may lie on your heart, dear wife, for these men are of your own blood, but it need never invade the hearthstone beside which I ask you to sit. The world will never know, whether you come with me or not, that Luttra Blake was ever Luttra Schoenmaker. Will you not then give me the happiness of striving to make such amends for the past, that you too, will forget you ever bore any other name than the one you now honor so truly?"

"O do not," she began but paused with a sudden control of her emotion that lifted her into an atmosphere almost holy in its significance. "Mr. Blake," said she, "I am a woman and therefore weak to the voice of love pleading in my ear. But in one thing I am strong, and that is in my sense of what is due to the man I have sworn to honor. Eleven months ago I left you because your pleasure and my own dignity demanded it; to-day I put by all the joy and exaltation you offer, because your position as a gentleman, and your happiness as a man equally requires it."

"My happiness as a man!" he broke in. "Ah, Luttra if you love me as I do you—"

"I might perhaps yield," she allowed with a faint smile. "But I love you as a girl brought up amid surroundings from which her whole being recoiled, must love the one who first brought light into her darkness and opened up to her longing feet the way to a life of culture, purity and honor. I were the basest of women could I consent to repay such a boundless favor—"

"But Luttra," he again broke in, "you married me knowing what your father and brother were capable of committing."

"Yes, yes; I was blinded by passion, a girl's passion, Mr. Blake, born of glamour and gratitude; not the self-forgetting devotion of a woman who has tasted the bitterness of life and so learned its lesson of sacrifice. I may not have thought, certainly I did not realize, what I was doing. Besides, my father and brother were not convicted criminals at that time, however weak they had proved themselves under temptation. And then I believed I had left them behind me on the road of life; that we were sundered, irrevocably cut loose from all possible connection. But such ties are not to be snapped so easily. They found me, you see, and they will find me again—"

"Never!" exclaimed her husband. "They are as dead to you as if the grave had swallowed them. I have taken care of that."

"But the shame! you have not taken care of that. That exists and must, and while it does I remain where I can meet it alone. I love you; God's sun is not dearer to my eyes; but I will never cross your threshold as your wife till the opprobrium can be cut loose from my skirts, and the shadow uplifted from my brow. A queen with high thoughts in her eyes and brave hopes in her heart were not too good to enter that door with you. Shall a girl who has lived three weeks in an atmosphere of such crime and despair, that these rooms have often seemed to me the gateway to hell, carry there, even in secrecy, the effects of that atmosphere? I will cherish your goodness in my heart but do not ask me to bury that heart in any more exalted spot, than some humble country home, where my life may be spent in good deeds and my love in prayers for the man I hold dear, and because I hold dear, leave to his own high path among the straight and unshadowed courses of the world."

And with a gesture that inexorably shut him off while it expressed the most touching appeal, she glided by him and took her way to the room where her father and brother awaited her presence.

CHAPTER XIX.

EXPLANATIONS

"I cannot endure this," came in one burst of feeling from the lips of Mr. Blake. "She don't know, she don't realize—Sir," cried he, suddenly becoming conscious of my presence in the room, "will you be good enough to see that this note," he hastily scribbled one, "is carried across the way to my house and given to Mrs. Daniels."

I bowed assent, routed up one of the men in the next room and despatched it at once.

"Perhaps she will listen to the voice of one of her own sex if not to me," said he; and began pacing the floor of the narrow room in which we were, with a wildness of impatience that showed to what depths had sunk the hope of gaining this lovely woman for his own.

Feeling myself no longer necessary in that spot, I followed where my wishes led and entered the room where Luttra was bidding good-bye to her father.

"I shall never forget," I heard her say as I crossed the floor to where Mr. Gryce stood looking out of the window, "that your blood runs in my veins together with that of my gentle-hearted, never-to-be-forgotten mother. Whatever my fate may be or wherever I may hide the head you have bowed to the dust, be sure I shall always lift up my hands in prayer for your repentance and return to an honest life. God grant that my prayers may be heard and that I may yet receive at your hands, a father's kindly blessing."

The only answer to this was a heavily muttered growl that gave but little promise of any such peaceful termination to a deeply vicious life. Hearing it, Mr. Gryce hastened to procure his men and remove the hardened wretches from the spot. All through the preparations for their departure, she stood and watched their sullen faces with a wild yearning in her eye that could scarcely be denied, but when the door finally closed upon them, and she was left standing there with no one in the room but myself she steadied herself up as one who is conscious that all the storms of heaven are about to break upon her; and turning slowly to the door waited with arms crossed and a still determination upon her brow, the coming of the feet of him whose resolve she felt must have, as yet been only strengthened by her resistance.

She had not long to wait. Almost with the closing of the street door upon the detectives and their prisoners, Mr. Blake followed by Mrs. Daniels and another lady whose thick veil and long cloak but illy concealed the patrician features and stately form of the Countess De Mirac, entered the room.

The surprise had its effect; Luttra was evidently for the moment thrown off her guard.

"Mrs. Daniels!" she breathed, holding out her hands with a longing gesture.

"My dear mistress!" returned that good woman, taking those hands in hers but in a respectful way that proved the constraint imposed upon her by Mr. Blake's presence. "Do I see you again and safe?"

"You must have thought I cared little for the anxiety you would be sure to feel," said that fair young mistress, gazing with earnestness into the glad but tearful eyes of the housekeeper. "But indeed, I have been in no position to communicate with you, nor could I do so without risking that to protect which I so outraged my feelings as to leave the house at all. I mean the life and welfare of its master, Mrs. Daniels."

"Ha, what is that?" quoth Mr. Blake. "It was to save me, you consented to follow them?"

"Yes; what else would have led me to such an action? They might have killed me, I would not have cared, but when they began to utter threats against you —"

"Mrs. Blake," exclaimed Mrs. Daniels, catching hold of her mistress's uplifted hand, and pointing to a scar that slightly disfigured her white arm a little above the wrist, "Mrs. Blake, what's that?"

A pink flush, the first I had seen on her usually pale countenance, rose for an instant to her cheeks, and she seemed to hesitate.

"It was not there when I last saw you, Mrs. Blake."

"No," was the slow reply, "I found myself forced that night to inflict upon myself a little wound. It is nothing, let it go."

"No, Luttra I cannot let it go," said her husband, advancing towards her with something like gentle command. "I must hear not only about this but all the other occurrences of that night. How came they to find you in the refuge you had attained?"

"I think," said she in a low tone the underlying suffering of which it would be hard to describe, "that it was not to seek me they first invaded your house. They had heard you were a rich man, and the sight of that ladder running up the side of the new extension was too much for them. Indeed I know that it was for purposes of robbery they came, for they had hired this room opposite you some days previous to making the attempt. You see they were almost destitute of money and though they had some buried in the cellar of the old house in Vermont, they dared not leave the city to procure it. My brother was obliged to do so later, however. It was a surprise to them seeing me in your house. They had reached the roof of the extension and were just lifting up the corner of the shade I had dropped across the open window—I always open my window a few minutes before preparing to retire—when I rose from the chair in which I had been brooding, and turned up the gas. I was combing my hair at the time and so of course they recognized me. Instantly they gave a secret signal I, alas, remembered only too well, and crouching back, bade me put out the light that they might enter with safety. I was at first too much startled to realize the consequences of my action, and with some vague idea that they had discovered my retreat and come for purposes of advice or assistance, I did what they bid. Immediately they threw back the shade and came in, their huge figures looming frightfully in the faint light made by a distant gas lamp in the street below. 'What do you want?' were my first words uttered in a voice I scarcely recognized for my own; 'why do you steal on me like this in the night and through an open window fifty feet from the ground? Aren't you afraid you will be discovered and sent back to the prison from which you have escaped?' Their reply sent a chill through my blood and awoke me to a realization of what I had done in thus allowing two escaped convicts to enter a house not my own. 'We want money and we're not afraid of anything now you are here.' And without heeding my exclamation of horror, they coolly told me that they would wait where they were till the household was asleep, when they would expect me to show them the way to the silver closet or what was better, the safe or wherever it was Mr. Blake kept his money. I saw they took me for a servant, as indeed I was, and for some minutes I managed to preserve that position in their eyes. But when in a sudden burst of rage at my refusal to help them, they pushed me aside and hurried to the door with the manifest intention of going below, I forgot prudence in my fears and uttered some wild appeal to them not to do injury to any one in the house for it was my husband's. Of course that disclosure had its natural effect.

"They stopped, but only to beset me with questions till the whole truth came out. I could not have committed a worse folly than thus taking them into my confidence. Instantly the advantages to be gained by using my secret connection with so wealthy a man for the purpose of cowering me and blackmailing him, seemed to strike both their minds at once, slow as they usually are to receive impressions. The silver-closet and money-safe sank to a comparatively insignificant position in their eyes, and to get me out of the house, and with my happiness at stake, treat with the honorable man who notwithstanding his non-approval of me as a woman, still regarded me as his lawfully wedded wife, became in their eyes a thing of such wonderful promise they were willing to run any and every risk to test its value. But here to their great astonishment I rebelled; astonishment because they could not realize my desiring anything above money and the position to which they declared I was by law entitled. In vain I pleaded my love; in vain I threatened exposure of their plans if not whereabouts. The mine of gold which they fondly believed they had stumbled upon unawares, promised too richly to be easily abandoned. 'You must go with us,' said they, 'if not peaceably then by force,' and they actually advanced upon me, upsetting a chair and tearing down one of the curtains to which I clung. It was then I committed that little act concerning which you questioned me. I wanted to show them I was not to be moved by threats of that character; that I did not even fear the shedding of my blood; and that they would only be wasting their time in trying to sway me by hints of personal violence. And they were a little impressed, sufficiently so at least to turn their threats in another direction, awakening fears at last which I could not conceal, much as

I felt it would be policy to do so. Gathering up a few articles I most prized, my wedding ring, Mr. Blake, and a photograph of yourself that Mrs. Daniels had been kind enough to give me, I put on my bonnet and cloak and said I would go with them, since they persisted in requiring it. The fact is I no longer possessed motive or strength to resist. Even your unexpected appearance at the door, Mrs. Daniels, offered no prospect of hope. Arouse the house? what would that do? only reveal my cherished secret and perhaps jeopardize the life of my husband. Besides, they were my own near kin, remember, and so had some little claim upon my consideration, at least to the point of my not personally betraying them unless they menaced immediate and actual harm. The escape by the window which would have been a difficult task for most women to perform, was easy enough for me. I was brought up to wild ways you know, and the descent of a ladder forty feet long was a comparatively trivial thing for me to accomplish. It was the tearing away from a life of silent peace, the reentrance of my soul into an atmosphere of sin and deadly plotting, that was the hard thing, the difficult dreadful thing which hung weights to my feet, and made me well nigh mad. And it was this which at the sight of a policeman in the street led me to make an effort to escape. But it was not successful. Though I was fortunate enough to free myself from the grasp of my father and brother, I reached the gate on — —- street only to encounter the eyes of him whose displeasure I most feared, looking sternly upon me from the other side. The shock was too much for me in my then weak and unnerved condition. Without considering anything but the fact that he never had known and never must, that I had been in the same house with him for so long, I rushed back to the corner and into the arms of the men who awaited me. How you came to be there, Mr. Blake, or why you did not open the gate and follow, I cannot say."

"The gate was locked," returned that gentleman. "You remember it closes with a spring, and can only be opened by means of a key which I did not have."

"My father had it," she murmured; "he spent a whole week in the endeavor to get hold of it, and finally succeeded on the evening of the very day he used it. It was left in the lock I believe."

"So much for servants," I whispered to myself.

"The next morning," continued she, "they put the case very plainly before me. I was at liberty to return at once to my home if I would promise to work in their interest by making certain demands upon you as your wife. All they wanted, said they, was a snug little sum and a lift out of the country. If I would secure them these, they would trouble me no more. But I could not concede to anything of that nature, of course, and the consequence was these long weeks of imprisonment and suspense; weeks that I do not now begrudge, seeing they have brought me the assurance of your esteem and the knowledge, that wherever I go, your thoughts will follow me with compassion if not with love."

And having told her story and thus answered his demands, she assumed once more the position of lofty reserve that seemed to shut him back from advance like a wall of invincible crystal.

CHAPTER XX.

THE BOND THAT UNITES

But he was not to be discouraged. "And after all this, after all you have suffered for my sake and your own, do you think you have a right to deny me the one desire of my heart? How can you reconcile it with your ideas of devotion, Luttra?"

"My ideas of devotion look beyond the present, Mr. Blake. It is to save you from years of wearing anxiety that I consent to the infliction upon you of a passing pang."

He took a bold step forward. "Luttra, you do not know a man's heart. To lose you now would not merely inflict a passing pang, but sow the seeds of a grief that would go with me to the grave."

"Do you then"—she began, but paused blushing. Mrs. Daniels took the opportunity to approach her on the other side.

"My dear mistress," said she, "you are wrong to hold out in this matter." And her manner betrayed something of the peculiar agitation that had belonged to it in the former times of her secret embarassment. "I, who have honored the family which I have so long served, above every other in the land, tell you that you can do it no greater good than to join it now, or inflict upon it any greater harm than to wilfully withdraw yourself from the position in which God has placed you."

"And I," said another voice, that of the Countess de Mirac, who up to this time had held herself in the background, but who now came forward and took her place with the rest, "I, who have borne the name of Blake, and who am still the proudest of them all at heart, I, the Countess de Mirac, cousin to your husband there, repeat what this good woman has said, and in holding out my hand to you, ask you to make my cousin happy and his family contented by assuming that position in his household which the law as well as his love accords you."

The girl looked at the daintily gloved hand held out to her, colored faintly, and put her own within it.

"I thank you for your goodness," said she, surveying with half-sad, half-admiring glances, the somewhat pale face of the beautiful brunette.

"And you will yield to our united requests?" She cast her eye down at the spot where her father and brother had cowered in their shackles, and shook her head. "I dare not," said she.

Immediately Mrs. Daniels, whose emotion had been increasing every moment since she last spoke, plunged her hand into her bosom and drew out a folded paper.

"Mrs. Blake," said she, "if you could be convinced that what I have told you was true, and that you would be irretrievably injuring your husband and his interests, by persisting in that desertion of him which you purpose, would you not consent to reconsider your determination, settled as it appears to be?"

"If I could be made to see that, most certainly," returned she in a low voice whose broken accents betrayed at what cost she remained true to her resolve. "But I cannot."

"Perhaps the sight of this paper will help you," said she. And turning to Mr. Blake she exclaimed, "Your pardon for what I am called upon to do. A duty has been laid upon me which I cannot avoid, hard as it is for an old servant to perform. This paper—but it is no more than just that you, sir, should see and read it first." And with a hand that quivered with fear or some equally strong emotion, she put it in his clasp.

The exclamation that rewarded the act made us all start forward. "My father's handwriting!" were his words.

"Executed under my eye," observed Mrs. Daniels.

His glance ran rapidly down the sheet and rested upon the final signature.

"Why has this been kept from me?" demanded he, turning upon Mrs. Daniels with sternness.

"Your father so willed it," was her reply. "'For a year' was his command, 'you shall keep this my last will and testament which I give into your care with my dying hands, a secret from the world. At the expiration of that time mark if my son's wife sits at the head of her husband's table; if she does and is happy, suppress this by deliberately giving it to the flames, but if from any reason other than death, she is not seen there, carry it at once to my son, and bid him as he honors my memory, to see that my wishes as there expressed are at once carried out.'"

The paper in Mr. Blake's hand fluttered.

"You are aware what those wishes are?" said he.

"I steadied his hand while he wrote," was her sad and earnest reply.

Mr. Blake turned with a look of inexpressible deference to his wife.

"Madame," said he "when I urged you with such warmth to join your fate to mine and honor my house by presiding over it, I thought I was inviting you to share the advantages of wealth as well as the love of a lonely man's heart. This paper undeceives me. Luttra, the daughter-in-law of Abner Blake, not Holman, his son, is the one who by the inheritance of his millions has the right to command in this presence."

With a cry she took from him the will whose purport was thus briefly made known. "O, how could he, how could he?" exclaimed she, running her eye down the sheet, and then crushing it spasmodically to her breast. "Did he not realize that he could do me no greater wrong?" Then in one yielding up of her whole womanhood to the mighty burst of passion that had been flooding the defenses of her heart for so long, she exclaimed in a voice the mingled rapture and determination of which rings in my ears even now, "And is it a thing like this with its suggestions of mercenary interest that shall bridge the gulf that separates you and me? Shall the giving or the gaining of a fortune make necessary the unital of lives over which holier influences have beamed and loftier hopes shone? No, no; by the smile with which your dying father took me to his breast, love alone, with the hope and confidence it gives, shall be the bond to draw us together and make of the two separate planes on which we stand, a common ground where we can meet and be happy."

And with one supreme gesture she tore into pieces the will which she held, and sank all aglow with woman's divinest joy into the arms held out to receive her.

I was present at the wedding-reception given them by the Countess De Mirac in her elegant apartments at the Windsor. I never saw a happier bride, nor a husband in whose eyes burned a deeper contentment. To all questions as to who this extraordinary woman could be, where she was found, and in what place and at what time she was married, the Countess had apt replies whose art of hushing curiosity without absolutely satisfying it, was one of the tokens she yet preserved, of her short sway as grand lady, in the gayest and most hollow city of the world.

As I prepared to leave a scene perhaps the most gratifying in many respects that I had ever witnessed, I felt a slight touch on my arm. It came from Mrs. Blake who with her husband had crossed the room to bid me farewell.

"Will you allow me to thank you," said she, "for the risk you ran for me one day and of which I have just heard. It was an act that merits the gratitude of years, and as such shall be always remembered by me. If the old French artist with the racking cough ever desires a favor at my hands, let him feel free to ask it. The interest I experienced in him in the days of my trouble, will suffer no abatement in these of my joy and prosperity." And with a look that was more than words, she gave me a flower from the bouquet she held in her hand, and smilingly withdrew.

Lector House believes that a society develops through a two-fold approach of continuous learning and adaptation, which is derived from the study of classic literary works spread across the historic timeline of literature records. Therefore, we aim at reviving, repairing and redeveloping all those inaccessible or damaged but historically as well as culturally important literature across subjects so that the future generations may have an opportunity to study and learn from past works to embark upon a journey of creating a better future.

This book is a result of an effort made by Lector House towards making a contribution to the preservation and repair of original ancient works which might hold historical significance to the approach of continuous learning across subjects.

HAPPY READING & LEARNING!

LECTOR HOUSE LLP
E-MAIL: lectorpublishing@gmail.com